Blood Ties

Ravenswood Crime Series

Tony Millington

CITY STONE
PUBLISHING

City Stone Publishing

ISBN (paperback): 978-1-915399-28-1
ISBN (ePUB): 978-1-915399-29-8

A CIP catalogue record for this book is available from the British Library.

Tony Millington | www.facebook.com/TonyMillingtonAuthor

City Stone Publishing | www.citystonepublishing.com

February 2024

To Mum

Joan Millington
1939-2023

PROLOGUE

DETECTIVE SERGEANT KEITH MONTEITH opened the door and walked to the headquarters' car park, glad his day had finished. Chief Superintendent Matthews had been pressing him again for information on the Russells, but he was getting nowhere with just being a patron of the casino. They kept their business and private lives separate. Trying to make a jerk like Matthews understand that was impossible.

Their new Detective Superintendent, Tanya Wright, turned out to be fair but tough; Detective Chief Inspector Watson, Detective Constable Lorimer, and he found they could work well with her.

Monteith was eager to spend some time with his family and relax for a couple of days before re-entering the madhouse that is policing. As he walked towards his BMW, he checked his phone. *Just the normal crap*, he thought.

His hand reached for the car door. Two men clad in dark clothes suddenly appeared in front of him.

Before he could react, one of them smashed a right-handed punch into his face. The force of the punch sent Monteith bouncing off the front of the car next to him. He groaned and stumbled, trying

1

to regain his senses. But before he could find the strength to get up, a hessian bag was put over his head and his hands were pulled back and bound behind his back.

'What the hell... Who are you?' he shouted, before screaming as the full force of a kick in the stomach took the wind out of him. He heard a van pull up next to him and doors opening. His attackers lifted him off the ground and threw him into the back. Doors were being slammed shut, and the engine revved as the van moved off.

———

Allan Russell watched from his car at a safe distance. *The hitmen were doing their job down to the letter.* It looked like Monteith did not know what hit him as the boys grabbed him and stuffed him into the van. He waited till the van had left the car park before he followed at a safe distance.

'Got you.'

———

Jimmy Russell was sampling one of the finest scotches in his collection, a Highland Park, distilled in 1974, and bottled in 2006. Only one hundred and forty-one bottles had ever been produced.

As he leaned back in his leather chair, his mobile beeped. It was a text message.

Your package has been collected

CHAPTER ONE

Monday 6:15 p.m.

DETECTIVE CHIEF INSPECTOR TERRY Watson had joined his family in Ravenswood's new dessert restaurant, celebrating the twelfth birthday of their son, Jason. He would have preferred something like a steakhouse, Domino's, or Frankie & Benny's, but he had been outnumbered.

It was the first time in months that they did something together as a family because of the recent high caseload. The serial killer they had been pursuing had finally been caught, and now Watson was able to let his hair down. He looked at his three children, Simon, Rachael, and Jason, and smiled contentedly.

The restaurant was packed and humming with noise from the early evening trade.

'Just grin and bear it,' his wife Sally whispered, as the kids were busy picking what they were going to have.

'Hope you have something better to eat back home after this?' he winked.

'I'm sure I can whip something up for you, dear.' Sally had a glint in her eye. 'Right, who is having what?' she said to the three excited faces looking back at her.

'Can I have a Hot Fudge Sundae?' Jason piped up.

'A Knickerbocker Glory, please Mum,' Simon gleefully added.

Little Rachael with her rosy cheeks was a study of concentration. Sally leaned over. 'What do you fancy?'

'I'm not sure... erm, Banana Split!' she grinned.

'Banana split it is then.'

Sally's phone rang as the waiter took their orders.

'Hello?' Sally struggled to hear the person on the other end with all the noise in the restaurant.

'Hi Sally, it's Katie. Sorry to ring you, but is Terry with you?' Katie was the wife of Terry's partner, DS Keith Monteith.

'Yes. Can you speak up? I can hardly hear you.' Sally tried to block out what noise she could.

'Keith is not home yet. I was wondering if Terry knew where he was.' Katie sounded worried.

'I will pass you across,' Sally shouted before giving the phone to Terry. She mouthed Katie's name.

'Just a minute, Katie.' He took the phone and went outside. The buzz in front of the restaurant was just as bad, so he nipped down a side alley.

'Hi Katie, I can hear you now. Jason says thanks for his present, by the way. Keith? No, he was still at the office when I left, finishing some paperwork. DSI Wright was also still there.' Terry heard his own phone ringing in his pocket. He looked at the screen. *Talk about the devil.*

'Katie, I am sure he will be home soon. You know what he is like for forgetting the time. Listen, speaking of our boss, I've got her on the line. I'll check in with her and get back to you.'

He changed phones.

'Hello, ma'am.'

'Sorry to pull you away from Jason's party, but can you get back here now? We have a big problem.' He heard a click. DSI Wright had hung up.

He felt bewildered. Had he forgotten to do something? One of his team? What was going on?

Returning to the restaurant, he bent over to Sally and whispered that he had to go back. As expected, her face was like thunder. He hastily said goodbye to his children, who did not look too disappointed. *A good thing they were waiting for their treats*, he thought.

Ten minutes later and out of breath because he'd been running most of the way, Watson joined Wright and Detective Constable Lorimer in the CID office.

An agitated Chief Superintendent Matthews and Custody Sergeant Bill Makepiece were already present. Everyone was looking at CCTV footage of the police car park at the back of their headquarters. The footage showed Monteith exiting the custody door, head down, looking at his phone, followed by being confronted and attacked by masked two men who bundled him into the back of a dark-coloured van and took off.

'Why did we miss this? Why didn't someone help him?' DSI Wright shouted.

Makepiece looked defeated. 'We were busy. All the cells are full down there and it was kicking off. The first thing anyone knew was when I glanced at the CCTV and saw Keith being chucked into the van. By the time we got out there, the van was gone,' he defended himself.

'Right, we have all squad cars on the lookout for the van with an "approach with caution" order. We don't want to put DS Monteith in any bigger harm than he is already in,' Wright informed them. 'A call has gone out for the helicopter to give us eyes in the sky.'

'Who has he pissed off lately?' said Matthews.

Tactful as ever, thought Watson. His resentment grew. 'No one!' he banged his fist on the desk. 'After you ordered him to get close to Jimmy Russell, he tried to get his life back together. He has kept his head down and got on with his work.'

'Watson!' Wright said sternly. 'My office. Now.'

'Just remember who you're talking to, DCI Watson,' Matthews snapped. Watson was about to respond but caught Wright firmly shaking her head; instead, he fixed his eyes on Mathews and thought, *You're a fucking idiot*, before briskly marching into Wright's office.

'I suggest you keep your troops in check, DSI Wright.' Matthews pointed a finger at her before turning and walking out of the door back to his office on the top floor.

Watson, still angry, flexed his fingers and loosened his neck muscles while looking out of the window at the city centre. As Wright entered, he turned to face her, and she closed the door.

'Don't say anything,' Wright told Watson off. 'Do not ever fly off the handle like that. What were you thinking?'

'I'm sorry, ma'am, but Matthews is a moron. He does not have a clue. Having a go at Keith like that was out of order, especially when he's out there...'

'I feel the same about Monteith, but shouting in Matthews' face does not help. They warned me when I took this job what he was like, and he does have his head up his arse, stuck up there in his office. But there are ways and means to keep him off our backs.'

Watson couldn't help but grin. Sniggering, he looked at his boss and they both laughed. DSI Wright had been a breath of fresh air with her easy-going nature. Professional when need be, and always backed her people up to the full.

Calming down, Wright continued, 'Now, I know Keith is a good friend, but let us think rationally. Keith has a not-so-clean past, so has there been any recent incident which may have led to him being bundled into a van as we saw? What about the Russells?'

He sighed and sat down. 'Abduction is not normally their thing. Keith paid his dues to them before you took over. Intimidation and power building have been their style, but they have kept a low profile lately. Not putting their heads above the parapet. According to Keith, they were expanding their casino business. Possibly adding a so-called private gentleman's club.'

'Do they need planning permission for that?'

Watson shrugged. 'Who knows? And will they care if they do? They will get around it somehow. Just mention the Russell name and watch everyone either run a mile or lick their shoes. They have this city tied up.'

A knock on the door. Lorimer entered. 'Sorry to interrupt, nothing from the squad cars, but the helicopter crew has just reported seeing a large vehicle on fire out by the landfill site. With it getting dark, they cannot be certain if it's the one we are after. Fire engines have arrived. The heli will continue searching unless told to stand down.'

'Hang on Karl. Terry, you and Karl check that out and report back. We need to be certain it is our van or rule it out.' Wright followed them back into the central office. 'Take a print-out of the CCTV picture of the van we are after.'

Putting on his jacket, Watson suddenly remembered Katie's phone call. 'Shit, what about Keith's wife? When are we going to tell her that her husband's gone missing? She rang me just before you did, asking if I knew where he was.'

'Check the van first. Can your wife go round there just to check on her and be there with her if we have news?'

Watson nodded, 'Good idea, ma'am. I'll call her.'

Monday 8 p.m.

Please don't be in there. I couldn't take it... Watson's mind was swirling with panic. *No, no, please no.* He could see visions of his friend's burnt body lying in the van. He looked at Lorimer, driving, his face contorted with concentration.

With their blues and twos on, they arrived at the wasteland by the landfill in no time. Both had been listening to the airwaves for updates, keeping their chat to a minimum, afraid to venture their thoughts. Watson thought of Katie and of Sally, on her way to Katie.

The van was smouldering, and thick smoke hung overhead like another layer to the cloud formation in the night sky, mixed with the stench of the fermenting waste from the landfill. Both covered their mouths with hankies and showed their ID cards to the PC on duty, who directed them over to the fire chief.

'What brings you lot out to a van fire?' The fire chief looked surprised.

'One of our colleagues has gone missing, taken in a van similar to this one,' Watson replied tersely.

'And you think they are in there? Jesus!' the chief exclaimed. 'There's no hope for them. It was well ablaze when we arrived. We are dampening down, but we can check soon. Just give us some time.'

Half an hour later, they were allowed to approach the burnt-out remains. Nothing of significance looked to have remained. No number plates, no identification.

'Fire was definitely started with an accelerant. Probably petrol,' the fire chief confirmed. 'But that's not what you are here for.'

Both Watson and Lorimer were shown around the van, keeping at a safe distance in case of flare-ups, to the sliding side door. It was open.

'Whoever did this doused the insides of the van with the petrol before setting it alight. There looks to be nobody inside the van. Even with a fire of this intensity, you would still see remnants.'

As Lorimer returned to the car to report their findings to DSI Wright, Watson took one of the fireman's torches and inspected what was left inside — which was not much. The fire had done its job. Heat was coming off the van and the surrounding air. His face and hands felt like they were on fire.

'Let us know if you come across anything of interest.' Immensely relieved, he handed back the torch.

'We picked up half a number plate from outside of the van.' The fire chief handed it to Watson. 'Don't know if it came from the van or from another vehicle. The front number plate has gone up in flames.'

'That's not enough to do a PNC check.' The plate only had AC15 on it. 'A lot of cars and vans would have the same on their plates. Bag it and give it to forensics when they arrive, thanks.'

Watson slowly walked back to the car. *Where the hell are you, Keith?* Taking out his phone, he tried Monteith's number again, leaving another voicemail.

———

Lorimer dropped Watson off at Monteith's house around 9 p.m. Before he'd had a chance to knock, the front door flew wide open. Katie looked at him anxiously.

'Terry?' Katie shot out past him into the street. 'Where's Keith? Sally said you went out to find him. Where is he?' she screamed before breaking down in tears.

Sally took her in her arms and guided her back through to the front room. Watson closed the door behind him. Jason appeared at the top of the stairs. He told him to stay up there and to keep everyone busy. Before entering the living room, Watson took a deep breath. This was going to be tough.

Sally had sat Katie down on the leather settee. He sat in an armchair. Katie looked up at him and mouthed, 'Where is he? Is he dead?'

Watson sat forward and looked at his hands, clasped together between his knees. 'Keith was signing off on some paperwork with our boss when I left. He left shortly after, and when he walked to his car, he was attacked by two people in masks. We have seen that on CCTV. They grabbed him and threw him into a dark-coloured van that left the car park. We have cars out and a helicopter to track down that van. Everybody is out there looking for Keith. We will not stop until he is found.'

He shrugged, feeling inadequate. Why hadn't they found Keith yet? He felt they should have. *Where are you, Keith? In a ditch somewhere with a bullet in your head?*

Katie's sobs brought him back to reality. She stared at him blankly. He could not tell if what he had said had registered. Her eyes seemed vacant. A couple of times he thought she looked like she was going to say something, mouth opening, but nothing came out.

He lent forward, putting a hand on her knee. 'Katie? Did you hear what I said?'

'Do you have any idea who took him or why?'

'We don't know. There were no visible markings on the van, and the CCTV could not pick up the number plate. I am speaking as a friend now, was there anything out of the ordinary lately? Something Keith said or did that seemed off?' He knew he was clutching at straws.

'Like what?'

'I don't know. How has he been?'

'Normal,al I think, as far as normal goes with Keith.' Katie rocked back and forth, her hands clasped around a tissue resting on her knees. 'We had thrashed out the business with that bastard Jimmy Russell. Keith said he was done with the gambling business and would not go near it. As far as I know, he has not been near that bloody casino. But we all know he has said that before.' She was close to tears again.

They looked at each other, remembering his past lies which had almost wrecked the couple's marriage.

He hated prying into their life, but he pressed on.

'Apart from the Russell business, how has he been at home?'

Katie shrugged. 'He's been the dutiful husband. Home at normal times except when he is on late duty with you. Takes care of the kids. Oh my God, what am I going to tell them?' She rocked to and fro.

Sally rubbed Katie's shoulder and looked over at her husband and shook her head.

'Please, Terry, Katie has obviously no idea. Why don't you go back to the office, and I'll let you know if Katie comes up with anything.'

He reluctantly agreed and said goodbye.

Sally followed him to the door. 'I will stay with her and ask mum to look after the kids for the night. Keep me updated by text. I will tell Katie anything she needs to know.'

Watson kissed and hugged Sally, knowing Katie would be in safe hands.

'A moment longer,' Sally held him and quickly added, 'And while you are at it, go home and change. You smell of smoke.'

Monday Night

DS Keith Monteith slowly came to. He felt the cold and hard floor beneath his body. His head pounded like it had a hundred wild horses running through it. His body ached like he had gone one round with a heavyweight boxer. *A broken rib or two?* Opening his eyes, he couldn't see anything, but he could still smell the hessian and feel the rough fabric against his head. He tried to move his hands, but found they were tied behind his back. The tie wraps bit fiercely into his wrists. His palms felt crusty. The ties had drawn blood.

How the hell did I get here? Think, damn it. Focus. Remember. Shit. How long have I been trusted up like a pig? I'm going to kill the bastards. Shit, my head, my body, the fucking pain. Where was I? Leaving work? Yes, that's it. I was walking to my car, getting into it. No, I didn't. Why? They came out of nowhere. Who? Concentrate. This bloody headache. I was attacked, yes. By whom? I never saw them. I'm still alive, I'm still alive. Thank God I'm still here.

His mind was a blank canvas. His frustration grew. *Shit, shit, shit.*

Am I alone or is someone watching me? Listening, he tried to hear anything that could help him. Noise, talking, machinery, transport... There was nothing but silence.

'Help! Is anyone there? ANYONE?' He immediately regretted it. *Shit, my head. Stop the horses. Stop the Grand National.*

He waited until the pain subsided. Shuffling his body around, he tried to sit up. The hessian bag made it practically impossible to see, so laying on his back, he rolled towards what he hoped would be one wall of the room he was in. After a few rolls, he banged into one. It sent shockwaves through his already bruised and battered body. *Aagghh, shit, shit.*

A vision of Katie came through. He felt alone. *Katie, Rebecca, and Pixie, I love you all. Christ, have they reported me missing? Has anyone? Is anyone looking for me? Terry, Lorimer, the boss? Did anyone see what happened? Katie, I love you, darling.*

He realised whoever had taken him had removed his phone, car keys, and wallet from his pockets; he had not felt them as he'd rolled across the floor. His watch was also missing from his wrist.

Before he could work out how to get up off the floor, the decision was made for him. He heard the door being unlocked and opened. A bright light was switched on.

He was grabbed by the arms above the elbows and was dragged away from the wall and dumped onto what felt like a wooden chair.

'Take the bag off,' someone barked.

What, I recognise that voice, but where from? No, it couldn't be!

The hessian bag was forcefully removed from his head.

He squinted, opening his eyes to get them used to the full glaring light from the bulb overhead. When he stopped squinting, he could just make out his three abductors. Two he recognised as Jimmy Russell's goons, Lex and Ray, from his previous visits to Russell's casino. And the other belonged to the voice he had recognised: Allan Russell, Jimmy's older brother.

'If this is how you treat all of your guests, it's no wonder you're not on any of the travel sites,' Monteith said sarcastically. He soon regretted it. A punch to the stomach made him grumble. He winced.

Allan Russell walked over to Monteith and bent down. His face close. 'You are only still here and not dead and dumped in some ditch because of my brother. God only knows why.'

Allan stood back and gestured to Lex and Ray. 'Get our guest cleaned up. Can't keep my brother waiting.' He left the room, slamming the door behind him.

Monteith stared at Lex and Ray.

'Well, where's the shower then?' he grinned. 'You heard him. Can't keep the boss waiting.'

CHAPTER TWO

Tuesday 5 a.m.

DAWN WAS BREAKING OVER Ravenswood. The hesitant morning light cast an eerie shine in the office. It looked like a doss house. Police officers of all ranks using all the willpower they had to keep awake, twelve hours into the investigation. Coffee and tea mugs were littering the desks. As were the wrappers and bottles from various takeaways. Most of the officers were from the night shift, although some of the previous day's day shift had refused to stop searching. Either they had continued their shift, or came back after a break.

On the wall was a map of Ravenswood and surrounding areas, each of which was being crossed off after searching. After eleven hours, there hadn't been a positive sighting of Monteith. Hotel receptionists, B&Bs, people using the railway station, and the bus station were all given photos of Monteith, to no avail. As if he had vanished of the face of the earth.

In the room for DSI Wright's debrief were Watson, Lorimer, and two new CID arrivals: Detective Constables Emma French and Paul Sandall. A few uniformed officers had also joined them.

Gone was Wright's pristine look, smart clothes and neat hairdo. Now she was jacketless, blouse outside of her skirt, shoes off and hair untied and flowing around her shoulders.

Watson and Lorimer were in a worse state. After spending most of the evening and night on the lookout for their colleague and friend, they had collapsed in their chairs, utterly exhausted. After a quick visit to the locker area for a face swill and toilet break, they were back, awaiting the debrief.

Watson quickly checked his phone. Sally's last text appeared.

> 4.12 am Katie is finally asleep. Mum has the kids. Love you xx

He texted back.

> Morning. No sign of Keith, will update you later when know more. I love you xx

French and Sandall had been collecting all the information that flowed back from the search teams. Both were still wired from all the coffee and energy drinks they had consumed.

Wright, with dark rings around her eyes, brought the debrief to order. 'Okay, almost twelve hours ago we had one of our own taken from beneath our noses, and we still don't know where he is. Emma, Paul, can you bring us up to speed?'

Emma French began: 'We have covered most the city. We're waiting to hear back from the teams from outlying villages. Divers have been into the weir because someone thought they had seen a body. Turned out to be a mannequin dressed up.'

'Typical!' Lorimer grunted as he stifled a yawn.

Paul Sandall took over. 'We've searched what industrial units we could get into, both derelict and in use. Building sites and other disused buildings have all come up empty.'

'We did catch three lads breaking into the building site on St Peter's Street, and a van which was pulled over contained stolen goods,' the night duty sergeant added from the back of the room.

'Make sure you add them to your stats,' Lorimer replied sarcastically.

'Piss off,' the duty sergeant snapped. 'Don't forget you were one of us not so long ago.'

'Gentleman, leave the bickering out,' Wright cut in.

'Seriously, are we now thinking someone has him tied up somewhere, and he is unable to contact us?' Watson got up from his chair to stretch his legs. 'I tried his phone numerous times. Went to voice mail at first, but since just after eleven o'clock last night, it went dead. Probably out of battery.'

'So basically, we have bugger all!' Wright exclaimed. She massaged her temples, looking pained. 'Go and take a break and we will reconvene in an hour so we can set out a plan.'

On the other side of the city, Monteith was being escorted by Jimmy Russell's thugs, Lex and Ray, from the vaults of the casino. He smiled. *These two looked like gorillas dressed in suits two sizes too small for them. They need a better tailor.*

Jokes aside, he realised he was in deep trouble. Anybody else, and he'd have a chance to talk himself out of his precarious situation. Not with the Russells. *What the hell do they want?*

They used the back entrance to the casino. Cleaners were busy tidying up the mess from the evening before. Nobody turned to watch the procession. It was more than their job's worth.

From the floor, Lex and Ray took him through a private door and into a lift to the balconette where the offices were. Jimmy's was the biggest and the most opulent. Monteith knew it too well: he had been there recently, paying back his gambling debts.

In Jimmy's office, they shoved him on a leather-backed chair facing Russell's large desk. Lex and Ray stood close behind him.

Nervously, Monteith looked around, taking in the ornate wooden desk, oriental in decoration. The glass-fronted drinks' cabinet sat in the corner behind the desk. There was a floor-to-ceiling bookcase matching the desk. At the other end of the office was a three-piece, dark green leather suite set around a large oval glass coffee table. The carpet was plush and patterned. A large gold-mounted mirror decorated with dragons on the wall by the door. Pictures of both the Russell brothers schmoozing with the great and good of Ravenswood — councillors and company directors. Charity events and business gatherings at the best hotels. *Everything a pair of crooks could want.*

The main double doors to the office opened and Jimmy and Allan Russell walked in, deep in conversation, looking at sheets of paper in a manila file.

Jimmy glanced over and smiled. 'Ah, Mr Monteith! How are you?' He signed a sheet, gave the file to his brother, and sat down at his desk. Allan stood next to him.

'I'm okay, considering I have been abducted, beaten up, held a prisoner with my hands tied up and a bag over my head. Also, I have a concussion and broken ribs, thanks to these two goons.' Monteith wanted to sound sarcastic, but he was too angry.

Lex and Ray moved towards Monteith, but a small shake of Jimmy's head sent them back. Another signal and they were ordered out of the office.

'Accept my apologies. I only told my boys to ask you to come and see me. If they were a bit over-enthusiastic, I will have a word with them.' Jimmy's smarminess was oozing out of every pore.

Allan smirked.

Jimmy continued, 'You see Keith, I've got a proposition.'

'You could have just phoned me!' Monteith seethed. 'And what makes you think I am interested? I have paid off my debt. End of story. I'll keep away from here if that's what you want.'

'No, on the contrary, I want you to come and work for me. As my Chief of Security,' Jimmy Russell said.

I could have sworn you just said work for you. Monteith let out a little laugh. But both Jimmy and Allan weren't laughing. They just stared back at him. 'What!? You're joking. Why me?'

'Because contrary to popular belief, I do like you,' Russell said from behind his ornate wooden desk. 'The others on my payroll, like Lex and Ray, just pay lip service. I say "Jump," and they say, "How high?" I hear from my sources you have guts. You and your DCI, Terry Watson.'

Jimmy got up and poured himself a drink from the cabinet. Sitting back down, he continued, 'Come work for me. You can do a lot better. What do you make as a detective? £30,000, £40,000? I can treble that. You could have anything you dream of. Just look around you. All the wealth and trappings. Do you really want to be Detective Plod of the police the whole of your life? I have big plans for the growth of this place.'

Unsure if what he had been offered was for real, Monteith replied, 'Sell out to you?'

Jimmy laughed. 'Sell out? No. Call it better job prospects. Will you get a promotion any time soon? Not with your gambling background. I hear Matthews has marked your cards.'

'And if I say no?'

He saw Jimmy and Allan exchange glances and felt uneasy.

'I could make life very difficult for you and your family,' Jimmy finally said.

Enraged, Monteith flew out of his chair. 'You leave my family alone!' he bellowed. 'Don't you dare come near them.' Threats against himself were one thing; threaten his family was different.

'Now there's the fire in you I like.' Jimmy Russell held his hands up in mock surrender. He gestured. 'Come with me. I have something to show you.'

What? Where the hell are we going now?

Confused, he followed Jimmy onto the balcony overlooking the casino floor. Lex and Ray stopped chatting and stood back.

'Take a look at that, a proper look.' Jimmy held his arms wide. Lines of fruit machines as far as you could see. Roulette and poker tables. Blackjack, baccarat. A long bar down one side sectioned off from the main floor. On the other side, doors leading to a large restaurant. 'This is my dream. I want to expand this casino and I need someone to advise me. I had to fire the last security officer for not doing his job properly.' Turning to Monteith, he said, 'I want *you* to take over. You will report to Allan.'

'Why don't you bring in a security firm? Haven't you got one in your pocket?' Monteith looked into Jimmy's cold dark eyes.

'No. I like to keep security in-house and tight. Hence why I had to let the previous guy go.'

Monteith considered asking what happened to him, but thought better of it. 'I need time to think this over.' *I need my head testing...*

'You've got to the end of the week.' Jimmy smiled, playfully tapping Monteith's cheek. 'If not, things could get tricky for you.' He signalled to Lex and Ray. Grabbing Monteith by the arms, they marched him off.

Jimmy joined Allan back in his office. Allan was shaking his head.

'Hope you know what you are doing, Jimmy.'

'I always know what I am doing.' Jimmy smiled before taking a swig of his drink.

'But are you sure he doesn't know?'

Jimmy turned to Allan. 'Friends close, enemies closer.'

Tuesday Afternoon

Coming up to a roundabout, a squad car trawling around the industrial estate, noticed something propped against a tree. They did a full circuit and then pulled over.

'Looks like someone's playing silly buggers again,' PC Gary Barnes said to his partner, PC Paula Dixon. 'Did you hear about the dressed mannequin they pulled out of the weir?'

'Whatever it is, it just moved. Look!' Dixon pointed over as she was unclipping her seatbelt.

'Bet you it's a drunk,' Barnes said dismissively.

They got out, dodging the cars exiting the estate, and approached what looked like a large bag of rags. As they got closer they could hear muffled groans.

'Come on. You cannot sleep here on the roundabout it's not safe,' Barnes said to the human form slumped by his feet.

The bundle tried to speak but was incoherent.

'Hey, he's got a bag on his head. And his hands are tied.' Dixon knelt down to pull the bag off.

'Just a minute fella, I will get it off… Bloody hell!' she exclaimed.

Barnes looked excited. 'I'll radio it in. PC192 Barnes to control, over.'

'Control here, what's your status? Watson,'

'We have just found Detective Sergeant Keith Monteith.'

The ambulance arrived within minutes of the call and took Monteith to A&E. He complained of a severe headache and painful ribs. His wrists and ankles were cut by the tie wraps.

Wright, Watson and Lorimer rushed to the hospital. After parking up, they flew into the reception area and into the main A&E department, leaving stunned receptionists and patients in their wake.

'Who the hell are you?' a disgruntled doctor bellowed, blocking their way.

DSI Wright waved her ID at the doctor. 'We're here to see DS Keith Monteith. He was brought in a few minutes ago. We need to speak to him urgently.' She tried to look past the doctor to see where Monteith was while inching forward.

'I don't care if you are the Prime Minister. You don't come bursting in here. How dare you try to throw your weight around.' The doctor signalled security, and they were escorted to a private waiting area. Wait there, was the message. They shrugged.

'We cannot do anything right now,' Wright said, 'so Watson and Lorimer, go home. You've been on duty for about twenty-four hours nonstop now. Have some rest, a good night's sleep and come back refreshed tomorrow morning.'

When Watson got home, Sally had already put the kids to bed. Grabbing a cold drink before going upstairs, he stripped off and had a shower, getting rid of the grime of a long and worrying twenty-four hours. True, Keith had been found, but that was only just the start of it. They were still in the dark as to who had taken him and why.

He closed the curtains, set his alarm and laid back on the bed, waiting for Sally to join him. His mind had other ideas. His dreams landed him in the middle of the shoot out of a previous case, a serial killer. It was as if he was watching the scene from the side. *What could I have done to change the outcome*? He was still unsure, but it ate at him, having been powerless to prevent the tragedy.

CHAPTER THREE

Wednesday 5:30 a.m.

HE WOKE UP IN a sweat with the bed sheets all over the place. He sat up and wiped his damp brow with both his hands. Shivers ran through his body. Looking at the clock, he had only been asleep for a couple of hours. Sally was fast asleep next to him. He tried to lie down again but was too restless and didn't want to wake her. He quietly got up and went downstairs to make a coffee and a bacon bap, realising he hadn't eaten the night before. Another coffee was enough to give him the kick-start he needed. He decided not to wait until his children woke, but go into the office early. Catching Keith's kidnappers was top of the list. He left a note for Sally saying he would ring later.

Arriving at headquarters, he parked his battered Ford Focus next to Monteith's car. The dent was still in the BMW's roof, made by Monteith during his mad rage after being given a grilling by Matthews over his gambling.

'You are getting lax in your pride and joy, my friend,' he murmured before entering the custody area.

'Any news on Keith?'

'Don't know, Bill. Just going to find out now. I will let you know later.'

'Listen, I'm sorry I didn't react sooner...'

'It's ok. Keith would still have been taken even if you had. Don't worry. We have him back now. I'll update you later.' He made for the stairs and went up to the office.

It did not surprise Watson to find the office deserted this early. He went over to his desk and put his jacket over the back of his chair before booting up his computer. Something caught his eye in the boss' office as he glanced through the open door. A pair of feet, which as he moved closer, he realised belonged to his DSI. She was asleep in a chair with her feet on the coffee table. He smiled. *Better let her sleep. She'd earned it.*

'What *are* you doing, Watson?' DSI Wright said, opening an eye and grinning.

'Oh, sorry ma'am.' He smiled. 'Didn't want to disturb you.'

'I heard you come in.' Wright got up, wincing.

'How long have you been here? Did you go home?' he asked.

Wright stretched her arms. 'No, not been home. I stayed; in case we had an update from the hospital. I told the others to go home and have a good sleep. What time is it now?'

'Ten past six, still early. Come on, I'll treat you to something from the canteen.'

'You say the sweetest things, Terry Watson.' Wright laughed. 'Give me a couple of minutes to freshen up.'

He waited until she was ready. Together, they walked towards the canteen.

'What are you going to do about Keith when he comes back?' Watson asked, once having got their coffee and scrambled eggs on toast in front of them.

'Depends how he is,' Wright said in between bites. 'Ask him to talk us through what happened, then while we search for his abductors, probably tell him to take a few days off to recuperate. Ensure he attends counselling.'

'Good luck with that!' he joked.

Wright's face showed she thought the same way. 'Any ideas about who it could be?'

Watson took his time in replying, taking a slurp from his cup. 'If he has got himself into something else since the gambling fiasco, I haven't heard anything about it. And if he has, I don't know if his marriage will survive this time.'

'How long has he been married to Katie?'

'Well, their eldest, Rebecca, is ten, so twelve years.'

Wright polished off the last bit of toast before asking, 'And you?'

'Me and Sally? Coming up for fourteen years this year.'

Wright nodded. 'How long have you been a detective, Terry?'

Watson leaned back in his chair. His face creased as he tried to remember. 'Been here for five years. The last 18 months as Chief Inspector. Took my detective's exam 13 years ago. Why'd you ask?'

'Matthews is looking into bringing in a DI to the agency.'

'What? From outside the agency?' Watson exclaimed in surprise.

'Yes. Unless I can think of anyone who fits the bill to act up.' Wright raised her eyebrows and looked over her cup at Watson.

'Keith?' Watson almost fell off his chair. 'DI?'

Wright wiped her mouth with her serviette and pushed her plate to one side. 'Just a thought, Terry. You have been here the longest and I would like your input.'

'Well, for one thing, Matthews would never consider him for DI.'

'Why wouldn't he?'

'How long have you got?'

Wright smiled and finished her drink. 'Think of it this way. Lorimer is waiting to see if he has passed his detective sergeant's exam and the two others, French and Sandall, have only just arrived. Who would you want to oversee them when neither of us is in the office? Keith or another newcomer? Also, I think it could be good for Keith. Calm him down by taking Lorimer under his wing.'

Watson nodded. 'Could work, but that's if you can get Matthews to agree to it.'

'Leave Matthews to me.'

Wednesday 9 a.m.

The previous night's exploits had taken a lot out of everybody. Looking for a missing person is tough. When it was someone you knew, worked with, considered a friend, it was incredibly hard. Not knowing if they were alive. Not knowing if you would see them again.

Watson and Wright returned from the canteen to find Lorimer, Sandall, and French in situ. All three were checking CCTV footage from the previous day. Wright informed them that Monteith was still in hospital, and she was waiting for an update on his condition.

The office doors opened. In walked Monteith, battered and bruised. They stared, then cheered.

'Did everyone miss me?' he hollered, with a big smile that couldn't hide the bruises on his face. His wrists were bandaged.

'Bloody hell,' Lorimer exclaimed, as they all stood up and walked over to meet him.

'When were you released?' Wright asked. Monteith could see concern written on her face.

'I discharged myself. Fed up with the missus moaning that I should stop being a detective and get out of the service.'

'Where is Katie now?' Watson asked.

Monteith grinned. 'Gone home, thank God, in a taxi after dropping me off. I decided on the way home to come in to see you, much to her growing anger. She thought I was nuts discharging myself, never mind coming in. Only hope she has calmed down when I get back.'

He wobbled. Watson and Lorimer each took one of his arms and helped him across the office to his desk.

'I think I might have a little bit of a concussion and mind the ribs. Docs say I have cracked a couple,' Monteith said, trying not to laugh.

'And you discharged yourself,' Watson said, shaking his head. 'Why am I not surprised?'

Monteith grimaced in pain. 'I needed to tell you what happened.'

He turned to Wright. 'Ma'am, you had better get Matthews down here. He will want to hear this.'

She looked at him, puzzled.

'Two words. Jimmy Russell.'

Over the next hour, wincing and coming up for breath, Monteith took them through all that had happened.

'I think there were two in the back with me. I could not tell how long we were in the van. We stopped a couple of times. Then I was dragged from the van and put into another vehicle. I think it was a normal car. I felt the carpet under me, and it was cramped and dark. Just before I was put in the boot, a bright flash blinded me for a couple of seconds. I must have blacked out after that because when I came to, I was in a dark room.'

'We found a burned-out van by the landfill. Sounds like you were in that one,' Watson said.

In between breaks, Monteith continued and related his conversation with the Russells to them. Nobody around the table said a word. All of them looked grim. Murder in their eyes.

Wright turned to Matthews. 'That should be enough to raid and arrest the Russells for false imprisonment and ABH considering we've got the abduction on CCTV.'

'Yes, but they can say they knew nothing about what their henchmen have done.'

'We cannot let them get away with what they have done to Keith,' Watson exclaimed.

Everyone around the table nodded in agreement.

'And we won't. I understand your frustration, but let's just hang on and think,' Matthews said. He turned to Monteith. 'This is out of character, even for Jimmy Russell, which means whatever he wants you on the inside for is big. Not just for him, but also for us.'

Monteith nodded, 'I agree. Sir, I hate the Russells as much as everyone in this room, but I will not give this job up because Jimmy Russell threatened me.'

Watson shook his head. 'For him to offer Keith the job of Chief of Security... What *is* Russell up to? And why does he need Keith?'

'But isn't this the chance we have been waiting for, to get inside the Russells' empire? They have opened the door, so why don't we walk straight through?' Lorimer remarked.

'*You* bloody do it!' Monteith shouted. He looked at Matthews, who was staring out of the office window. Monteith could see the veins on Matthews' neck standing out.

'Will you walk into my parlour said the spider to the fly. Tis the prettiest little parlour that ever you did spy,' Watson half-whispered.

'What?' Wright looked up.

'Just saying it's like the story of the spider and the fly. Guess which one we are?'

'When does Jimmy want your answer?' Matthews asked.

'End of the week,' Monteith said curtly.

Matthews fixed his gaze on him. 'Would you be willing to take up his offer and report back to me?'

Monteith started shaking. He blurted out, 'Willing no. Not a chance. But considering the threats made to my family, do I have a choice? Go into hiding? He will still find me.' He slumped in his chair.

'I'll take that as a yes, then. DCI Wright and I will work out a scenario to make it look as if you've left the force so you can start working for Russell.'

Watson voiced his concern. 'I don't like it. It's too risky.'

Monteith mustered a smile.

'You can be his handler. If Keith gets in trouble, we will pull him out,' Wright said.

Monteith and Watson looked at each other. 'Agreed.'

CHAPTER FOUR

Two Weeks Later — Monday 8.30 a.m.

'RIGHT, MUM, I'M OFF,' Alison Grant called up the stairs of their three-bed semi in the Normanton part of Ravenswood. She was dressed in her running gear with her long brown hair tied back in a ponytail.

Her mother, Joan, leaned over the bannister at the top of the stairs with a shirt hanger in her hand. 'Are you doing your short or long run this morning, darling?'

'Short run today — should be back in an hour.' Alison stood on the bottom step so her mother could see her. Joan Grant started down the stairs. 'Your Aunty Debbie would have been so proud of you.'

'I know, Mum. That's why I'm running the city half marathon.' Alison squeezed her mum tightly. Both had tears in their eyes.

'Okay, stay safe.' Joan smiled as she said the same words she always used when anyone of the family left the house.

'Always do, Mum. I need to go. Marcus will be round later and we are going into town.' Alison had with her a small bottle of water. She put in her earphones, switched on the music on her phone, started the stopwatch on her wrist, and shut the front door behind her.

'Why do they have to grow up so fast?' Joan said as she looked at her reflection in the hall mirror before giving it a wipe with the duster.

Alison had always been a bundle of energy. She was sporty, played tennis, and loved running. The sports teacher at Saint Mary's Academy, Stuart Wilkins, had recognised it and promptly introduced her to the athletics team. She became a star at 800 metres and cross-country, winning or coming second in all her races. This brought her to the attention of the local athletics club, and she began training with Ian Fellows, who coached her on how to make the most of her burgeoning talent.

The death due to breast cancer of her beloved Aunt Debbie six months ago made Alison decide to run the local half-marathon and raise money for breast cancer research. Training most days, she increased the length of her runs until she could run the 13.1 miles in two hours.

Alison took the path in between two of the neighbouring houses, which led to an unmanned crossing over the railway tracks, and out over to the countryside at the back of her house. She was careful to look both ways along the two-track railway. The locals had tried to get a bridge built over the tracks, but it was turned down as being not cost effective; the frequency of the trains was minimal, so it would be a waste of money, the council had said.

On the other side of the crossing, the path came out onto the end of a country lane. When they laid the railway in the 1960s and built the housing estate in the 1980s, they reduced the length of the path. Railway workers now used it to park their vans when there was maintenance work to be done on the branch line. Also, to the annoyance of the locals, it was used as a dumping ground by fly-tippers.

Alison, with her music playing and concentrating on her running, was oblivious to the blue van with its bonnet open. The last thing she remembered was the sharp pain at the back of her head, and then her legs buckling from underneath her as she hit the stone-chipped road with a sickening thump. Everything went fuzzy and blurry as her mouth filled with the metallic taste of blood.

An old grey trainer that had previously been white was stuck deep in a hedge about halfway up. The red streaks of plastic on its side were faded, the laces frayed at the end after losing their aglet plastic coating. It had been there for months now, hung in the hedge, with grass and stinging nettles underneath so thick, that you couldn't see through. How it got there nobody knew.

The hedge was part of the border which separated a local farmer's field from industrial wasteland to the south of Ravenswood. The industry had come and gone in a stint, leaving the land and buildings to nature. Burned-out cars and vans, fridges, beds and three-piece suites of all sizes had been tossed onto the site. The kids used the mounds of earth and rubbish as a makeshift playground. BMX tracks and jumps were made. Stolen cars were driven around by underage drivers before they were set on fire. But over the last month, workers had begun to clear the land, bought by a local property developer, ready for the building of a new housing estate. The clearance had now been stopped.

Watson showed his badge to the uniformed officer at the gates of the industrial estate and parked his Ford Focus next to the Portakabin offices. Getting out, he noticed a group of workers in safety helmets, boots, and fluorescent jackets gathered around a tea wagon. The smell of bacon, eggs, sausages and fried onions cooking hit his nostrils and his stomach grumbled. The tea and toast from breakfast had long gone. He would make a point of stopping there on his way out.

Watson asked a worker where he could find the project manager and was directed to a double Portakabin. 'He hides out in the top one of those two over there.'

As he climbed the metal stairs, he could hear a raised voice. He saw a stout man talking into a phone.

'How the hell do I know? I've not been told... They've kept us away from the area. Some DCI Joker from the police is supposed to be coming. I'll let you know later...'

The man slammed the phone down and turned the air blue with swear words even Watson had never heard before. He knocked on the open door.

'Who the hell are you?'

'I'm the DCI Joker you are waiting for.'

'Shit.' The man stood, mouth open, before regaining his composure. 'Sorry you had to hear that. Pressure from the powers above to get this thing moving — pain in the ass they are. They should come down and do a day's proper work. We're already behind, and now this.' He shuffled sideways through the gap between his desk and the office wall and held his large hand out. 'Ray Wilson.'

'DCI Terry Watson. What happened this morning?'

Both men moved out onto the metal stairs. The view of the industrial estate, below and to their left, spanned a good couple of acres. A large industrial unit towered in the centre of the area. Police tape had been put up all the way around. Two uniformed officers were at the large front door. The forensics team was already there, dressed in their white overalls and face masks. Watson spotted the pathologist, James MacIntosh's van parked close by.

'Some lads were in there, cleaning it out before we pulled it down, trying to dig out the ramps and brake testers. It was once used as a garage and MOT place. In the process, a large chunk of cement from the floor came with it. A lad spotted carpet in the hole. He pulled at it and the body was underneath. That's when we called you....'

A Portaloo opened and a skinny lad, no more than nineteen years, came out.

'That's the lad who found it, Paul. He's been puking his guts up ever since.'

'You never forget the first dead body,' Watson replied with some sympathy, looking at the lad who bolted for the loo again. 'Right, I had better join my colleagues at the crime scene. Thanks, Mr Wilson.' Watson started down the stairs to his car.

Wilson stopped him. 'I will take you over in my van if you don't mind. Health and Safety. I need to get an update myself on how long this is going to take. Also, it will give my ears a rest from the boss' telephone calls.'

He locked the office and followed Watson down to the car park and directed him to a white Nissan Navarra.

'You will need this.' Wilson lobbed Watson a safety helmet.

The drive over was quick, and Ray Wilson parked up next to the police tape. He got out, but Watson stopped him from going any further.

'As this is a crime scene, I need you to remain here.'

'But I need to find out when we can get back to work. My neck's on the line!' Wilson exclaimed.

Watson extended his arms. 'I understand, but I cannot let you in. Look, I will have a word with forensics. That's all I can do.'

Watson dipped under the tape, leaving a frustrated Wilson kicking the tyre of his van. 'Keep an eye on him will you,' he ordered the constable guarding the main door. The constable nodded and stood a little more alert than before.

Watson put on the safety helmet and signed in, donning a pair of shoe covers, gloves, and a face mask. He made his way over to the forensics' tent in the far corner, thinking about his words about never forgetting your first dead person. He could remember all the bodies he had seen. They would come into his mind to haunt him when he least expected it. Flashbacks were a bastard.

James MacIntosh appeared, stretching his back.

'Having fun, Mac?' Watson joked as he made his way across to him.

Mac removed his mask, gulping in some fresh air. 'Hi there stranger, wondered if you'd be turning up for this one.' The stench of rotting flesh filled the air.

'You got a new aftershave, Mac?'

'You noticed. It's called Corpse. The essence of decomposition mixed with bloated gas and a smidgen of dead fly larvae. Does wonders for your love life.'

'Didn't know you had one,' Watson smirked. He looked towards the tent. 'What do we have in your tent of wonders?'

'Let me show you. You'll need to hold your breath, though.' Mac opened the tent flap and they entered.

'It's not as bad as the time we fished that bloated body out of the river.'

Mac nodded. 'No, this is a six on the gagging scale.'

An eight-by-six-foot hole had been dug around the carpeted and tied-up body.

'We have taken the normal pictures during the excavation to catalogue the evidence while the body was still in situ. Anything of interest found we bagged and tagged,' Mac continued. 'We are close to bringing the body out of there.'

'Female or male?'

'Don't know, to look at what was left of the face. With a couple of hundredweight of concrete poured onto it, they are not looking their best. Will be able to give you a proper rundown of age and how they died and approximate time of death at the post-mortem.'

Both Watson and Mac came back out of the tent, taking off their gloves and masks as they strolled towards the main door. Mac broke the silence.

'Have you heard from Keith?'

Watson looked into the distance. 'No, not since he resigned.'

'It surprised me, him doing that. I thought you two were as thick as thieves, excuse the pun?'

He struggled talking about his best friend. 'He had personal troubles during the Freeman case. Skeletons from his past haunting him. I think it just took too much out of him. He needed to get away from everything.'

'I heard his Mrs divorced him and took the kids?'

'I know she took the kids and moved out.' He had had enough of the questioning, so it was a blessing that they were at the entrance of the industrial unit.

Until Ray Wilson spotted them. 'When am I getting my site back?' he shouted.

'Who's that guy?' Mac asked as he unlocked his van.

'The site manager. He's getting hassle from his bosses over this. Not being able to carry on with the demolition.. He needs to know when you will be finished so they can get on.'

'Tell him not for the rest of the day at least.' Mac had a big grin on his face. 'Let's see how he reacts to that.'

Watson chuckled. 'It will give him a heart attack and you another body to deal with.'

'Jokes apart, it'll take about another couple of hours to get our body out of the ground and tidy up.'

'I have to get back. Let us know when you are starting the post-mortem.' Watson shook Mac's hands and turned to Ray Wilson.

Wilson looked enraged when Watson told him what Mac had said when they drove back to the main office. They parked up. Wilson stormed up the metal stairs to his office, slamming the door without giving Watson a second glance.

The smell from the tea wagon was overpowering. Grabbing a bacon and egg bap covered with tomato sauce and tea, Watson settled in his car. As he took a mouthful, his phone went off. Noticing it was DCI Wright, he quickly swallowed his mouthful of bap and answered.

'Morning, ma'am.'

'Where are you, Terry?' The DCI sounded worried.

'I'm still down at the Copeland Industrial Estate.'

'Will you be able to make it for the 10 a.m. morning debrief? We have a lot to catch up on.'

'Yes, ma'am that will be fine. I only need a few more minutes here.'

'Okay, see you soon.'

He finished his bap and took off.

The CID office erupted in laughter when Watson walked in. He startled. Fingers pointed at his chest. He looked down at his tie, covered in tomato sauce.

'Shit.' He smiled and bowed, acknowledging the banter.

'Where's ours, you tight bugger?' Lorimer shouted as he brought a large file back to his desk.

'Back at the tea bar, you still owe me for the one last week,' Watson shot back as he put his stuff down on his desk and took off his jacket.

'Bollocks, I paid you for that one.'

'When you two have finished, we have work to go through.' Wright had come out of her office and was standing by the list of ongoing cases on the board.

'Now before I start, Karl, will you come to the front, please?'

'What? Boss, we were only joking. I will pay Terry back, honestly.' Lorimer looked alarmed. 'Here Terry, here's a tenner.' He threw a folded note on Watson's desk.

Watson picked it up and examined it. 'Just checking it's not a forgery, or the moths haven't got at it while it was in your wallet'.

'Well, you will want what I have for you, Detective Sergeant Lorimer.' DSI Wright stood holding a brand-new ID card. 'I have just heard you have passed your sergeant's exam. Congratulations. With all the good work you have been doing, I hope you will stay with us.'

The room again erupted, this time in cheers and whoops. A lot of back-slapping, and congratulations for Lorimer, as he shook hands with everyone. The last was Wright, as she hooked the lanyard containing his new card around his neck.

'Right then, simmer down. Let's get on. Terry, can you start with this morning's call?' Wright asked.

'Got called out to the Copeland Industrial Estate where a body of unknown gender was found by workmen demolishing the industrial units. It was buried under the concrete floor of the last remaining unit. The place had previously been used as a garage and MOT service centre. Mac was there when I turned up but had not removed the body yet. The post-mortem will be tomorrow at the earliest.'

'Isn't that where they are going to build that new housing estate?' Sandall asked. 'Looked very plush from the drawings I have seen.'

Watson couldn't keep the smile from his face. 'Yes. I spoke to a frustrated site manager, Ray Wilson. He was getting an ear bashing from the new owners who want the work to begin ASAP. He was not thrilled when we told him he might not get his site back until tomorrow.'

The DSI turned to Lorimer. 'Right, *DS* Lorimer, what are you working on?'

Another round of cheering and slapping of desks.

'Stolen debit cards.'

'Don't get caught now you're a DS.' Watson couldn't help himself.

'As I was saying,' Lorimer started again. 'A group of fraudsters is targeting the town centre with stolen bank cards, buying small-priced items under £100, so they don't need to confirm the purchase with a pin. They have been hitting supermarkets, games shops, and entertainment stores. We are waiting for the stores' CCTV coverage.'

'If you need any help on that, DC French can join you in looking through the images,' Watson added. French nodded and looked over at Lorimer.

'DC Sandall, you've been on these burglaries?' Wright asked..

'Yes, distraction burglaries. There have been four over the last week that we know of. We have asked the victims to do photo fits of the men involved. We can get pictures out to the press within an hour of completion.'

'Right, let's get on then. Terry, can you join me, please?' DSI Wright signalled for Watson to follow her into her office. She had already sat down behind her desk when he was near entering.

'Can you shut the door behind you, please?'

As instructed, he sat down on the chair in front of Wright's desk, which offered a view of the city through the window.

'I just wanted a chat to see how you are.' Wright leant back in her chair and looked at him.

He rubbed an imaginary hair from his trousers, wishing he was somewhere else.

'You haven't been going to see the counsellor recently, have you?'

He finally plucked up the courage to say something, but Wright put her hand up.

'I've been checking because you're a valuable and experienced member of this team.'

'It's not working for me, all this talking about my feelings.'

'After what happened in your previous case and to my predecessor... things like that leave a stain.'

'Is that speaking from experience, ma'am?' Watson hoped to deflect the conversation away from his feelings.

'We are talking about you, not me.' Wright looked uneasy. She got up and poured a glass of water. With her back to him, she asked, 'How are you sleeping?'

'Not brilliant, still getting flashbacks to the car park, wondering if I could have prevented it.'

'Don't punish yourself.' Wright turned to face him. 'From what I have been told, and reading all the reports, you did all you could to prevent the shooting. Nothing was going to stop the killer. They had clearly had made their mind up. If you had got in the way, you would not be here sitting in front of me.'

By her calm and measured voice, he knew she was trying to console him, but he was not having any of it.

'Try telling that to my brain at 3 a.m.,' he fired back.

Sitting on the edge of her desk, Wright said, 'That's what the counsellor is for Terry. See him, please.'

'Is that all, ma'am? I have a job to do.'

'Yes, that's all,' Wright sighed.

As they came out of the office, Lorimer was deep in conversation on his phone.

'Gov, we have a missing person,' Lorimer got up and showed the details to DCI Watson

'A seventeen-year-old female, Alison Grant, went for her normal morning run at about eight and has not returned. Said she would be an hour and now it's almost noon. Family and her boyfriend have been looking along the route she always takes and there is no sign of her.'

'How about friends?' Sandall queried. 'Did she stop off at someone's?'

'The family have spoken to them and none of them have seen her. Besides, they don't live on the route,' Lorimer replied.

Watson scanned over the details on the paper. 'Okay, DC French, you with me and we will interview the family. Get as much information on the young woman as we can.'

'I will arrange for a family liaison officer to join you,' the DSI added.

The blue van pulled into the driveway of the farmhouse. The countryside around the east side of Ravenswood was flat and inhospitable. Houses were sparse; with most neighbours so far away, you needed binoculars to see them.

The driver got out of the van, checking his passenger was still with him, before making his way to the house, unlocking the front door. He was carrying his work bag and a tool bag. He put his tool bag by the front door and switched on the hall light before carrying the other bag into the kitchen.

He had lived on his own for a couple of years. The farmhouse had belonged to his late parents. He'd not married, spending time helping on the farm and setting up his joinery and fencing business. He rarely ventured into Ravenswood city centre. The farmhouse and one small warehouse were all that was left after he had sold off the land to adjoining farmers.

After a drink, he went back out to the van and unlocked the back doors. Inside, on a mattress, legs and wrists tied, her mouth covered with tape, was his passenger. Picking her up, he carried her over his shoulder into the house. He opened the wooden door under the stairs, clicked on the light, and steadily ascended the ten steps. At the bottom was a hallway with pictures on the walls. Two bare light bulbs hung from the ceiling, one at each end. At the far end was a padlocked door. Pulling the key out of his pocket, he opened it to reveal a small room.

He carefully laid the young woman down on a mattress. She was still unconscious, her hair sticky with blood, her face and hands covered in cuts. The knees of her tracksuit were torn.

Taking out the old Nikon camera, he started snapping photos of her. When he finished, he knelt down and cut off a chunk of hair. Standing, he made his way to the other end of the room. Three shelves had been erected on the wall, each with small plastic see-through boxes on it. He removed an empty box and placed the young woman's hair into it. Marking it with a name and date, he added it to his collection.

CHAPTER FIVE

MONTEITH RELUCTANTLY OPENED HIS eyes. He was flat out on his stomach on his bed, fully clothed. The bedside light was still on, even though it was now daylight. Moving the half-drunk can of beer away, he glanced at the clock: 12.30 p.m. Sitting up, he switched the bedside light off only to find that he had also left the hall light on. He vaguely recalled getting in about 4 a.m. from the casino, but that was it..

He stripped off and stepped into the shower. Twenty minutes later, he had washed and changed. Downstairs, remnants of a Chinese takeaway and two beer empty beer cans were on the table in the living room. He frowned, unable to remember anything.

In the kitchen, he switched on the local radio station while he cleaned the Chinese and beer away. The one o'clock news was reporting about a girl who had gone missing, a gang of fraudsters in the city, and something about burglaries.

I should be in the thick of it, dealing with the bread-and-butter things of the department. He thought back to the dressing down he had with Superintendent Matthews. *Why the hell didn't I tell him to stick this undercover lark where the sun doesn't shine? I am risking my life trying to get information about the biggest and most dangerous crook in the city, Jimmy Russell. All for what? So Mr High-and-Mighty can get his face on the news and in the papers. Screw you, Matthews.*

He grimaced, knowing too well that the choice hadn't been his in the first place. Russells' threat against his family had been clear. He sighed. The house was too quiet. He missed Katie and the girls; she'd taken them to her mother and was ready to divorce if he did not stop this undercover assignment. He hadn't told her about the threats against her and the girls. She'd be safer not knowing, and not living with him. Threats against himself were one thing, against his family was different. The only way he could give Katie back her old husband, was finishing this job. Putting the Russells behind bars. For the moment, though, he felt much like the Aerosmith song "F.I.N.E.": Fucked Up, Insecure, Neurotic and Emotional. Yep, he was fine.

Watson and French pulled into the road where the Grants' house was. He parked behind the police car which had been sent when the first call of the missing girl came in. He looked at the house's front bay windows and frowned. Through the windows, he saw what seemed like a big argument. He could decipher a man and woman and some other people. Fingers were being pointed and arms flew.

DC French went to get out. Watson put a hand on her arm.

'Hang on. Let's see how this plays out.' He nodded towards the house. 'Normally, I would go straight in, but it looks like there is a blame game ongoing. We don't want to get caught in the middle of that.'

French looked at the house. 'Yes, sir, I see your point.'

A PC got out of the squad car and walked towards them.

'How long has this been going on, constable?'

'PC Gary Barnes, sir. About five minutes, as soon as the man arrived. That's his car on the driveway, the silver Mercedes. I was talking to the mother, Joan Grant, when he turned up.'

'I take it that's the husband?' French asked.

'Yes, a David Grant. He was not happy and brusquely asked me to leave, saying why was I not out looking for his daughter.'

'A charmer then!' French snorted.

'Who else is in there?' Watson asked, while keeping his eyes on the house.

'Their son, Alex, and Alison's boyfriend, Marcus Devonport,' Barnes read from his notes.

'I think it's time to meet the happy family,' Watson said as he walked towards the drive of the house. He glanced inside the Merc and spotted a briefcase with a newspaper sticking out. Today's *Times*. Before they reached the door, Joan Grant already opened it. Tears were streaming down her cheeks as she forced a smile of welcome.

'Have you found her?'

'I'm sorry, no, ma'am. I'm Detective Chief Inspector Watson, and this is my colleague, Detective Constable French. You have already met PC Barnes. Are you up to answering some questions?'

Joan Grant nodded and held the door open. Watson tried to smile at Joan, but to him, it seemed a hollow gesture.

In the living room, introductions were made, and everyone settled down. Apart from David Grant, who stood by the French windows looking out to the back garden. Watson observed him; he could practically feel the anger and frustration radiating off the man.

'Mrs Grant, can you tell us what happened this morning?'

His face red with rage, David Grant snapped, 'Our daughter went missing this morning. Why are you questioning us when you should be out there looking for her?

'DAVID, PLEASE.' Joan Grant turned apologetically to Watson. 'Sorry, my husband thinks he can order everyone around like he does at work.'

French took out her notebook as Joan Grant clearly tried to compose herself.

She took a deep breath. 'Alison said goodbye to me about eight thirty. She said she was doing her short run of about an hour. She's training for the city half marathon. Running it for breast cancer. By eleven o'clock, she was not back. When Marcus, her boyfriend, arrived, he went looking for her, while I rang her friends just in case she met up with someone. Marcus came back with nothing, so we rang the police.' She sobbed.

Alex put an arm around his mother. David Grant stood motionless.

Watson turned to Marcus, who was standing by the front window. 'How often does she go running, Marcus?'

'With the half marathon coming up, four times a week now. Sometimes short and some long,' Marcus explained while looking at his phone, 'I'm still hoping this will ring and Alison says she's alright and can I pick her up.'

Joan glanced up but said nothing.

'Might she have changed her mind and done a long run?'

Marcus shook his head. 'No, no. Alison always sticks to a routine. Short, long, short, long. Today was definitely a short run.'

Watson nodded. 'What do you get when you call her?'

'It just rings out, then goes to voicemail. Alison uses it to listen to music when running.'

Watson turned to Joan. 'How old is Alison?'

'Seventeen,' Joan replied in a broken voice.

He exchanged glances with French. 'Do you have a recent photo of Alison? Does she use Facebook or other social media?'

'I have some on my phone you can use.' Marcus flicked through his pictures. 'I took a couple last night when we were in town.' He leaned over the sofa, showing French a photo. 'That's Alison on the right, in the purple top.'

'Can you send them to my email address please?' French gave Marcus her card.

He tapped on his phone. 'Done.'

There was a knock on the front door. Watson asked Barnes to answer it. He re-entered with a female police officer.

Watson smiled. 'Mrs and Mr Grant, I'd like to introduce Police Constable Sharon Walsh. She's our family liaison officer and will stay with you. Any information we, or you, have, PC Walsh will act as a go-between.'

'WHY?' David Grant exclaimed. 'So you can spy on us? Do you think we've got something to hide?' he spat at Watson.

'No, PC Walsh is here to help you. If you can remember something that could be useful, PC Walsh will inform us. And if we need to pass anything to you, it will come via her.' He looked at

David Grant and the whisky glass in his hand. 'I trust you will not be driving anymore today, Mr Grant.'

'Thank you, Detective Chief Inspector,' Joan Grant intervened, glaring at her husband. 'We appreciate it.' She turned to PC Walsh. 'Sharon, is it? Welcome. Do you want coffee or tea?'

Watson signalled his intention to leave for Barnes and French. 'I think we'll be off.' Passing Marcus, he lent in. 'Marcus, walk me to the car, please.'

They walked out. Marcus made another call to Alison's phone, which went straight to voicemail.

'Mrs Grant said you went along the route Alison did for her short run?' French asked.

'Yes, she went out onto the country lanes via the cut through there. It leads over the railway.'

'How long have you been seeing Alison?'

'We have been together for about eighteen months, met at school.'

'Has there been any trouble at home?'

Marcus shook his head. 'No, none that Alison told me of. Her dad can be a pain as you saw, but if you think he's done something to Alison...' his voice trailed off. 'No way.'

'So, she wouldn't have just taken off and disappeared. She did not tell you she was leaving?'

'No, she would have told me, and if she had, I would have tried to talk her out of it.'

Barnes' radio sprung into life. He answered, and then turned to Watson. 'Sorry, I have to assist with an RTA nearby.'

'No worries, we have finished here,' Watson told him. 'You get off. Thank you for your help.'

———

Watson concentrated on the traffic building up around the Rhubarb roundabout on their way back to the police station. He looked at French, who seemed poised to say something. 'What is on your mind, French?'

'Well,' she hesitated. 'What did you think of that, sir?'

'Something's not right. We need more information, but I don't think Alison has run away.' He sounded sombre. 'Hopefully, Sharon can get Joan Grant to trust her.'

He signalled while switching lanes. 'Let's have another interview with Marcus, away from the family. Maybe he can come up with something that will help us locate Alison. Also,' he continued, 'we need to put out a bulletin on Alison's disappearance. Contact the press office. And get a couple of squad cars to search the route Marcus gave us. She may be in a ditch somewhere injured.'

Back at the CID headquarters, French set to work on the tasks while Watson brought DSI Wright up to speed.

They arranged for a sweep of the area by uniformed officers. French passed the photos of Alison on to the local media, with the headline:

Urgent. Missing Teenager

Watson and Wright were refilling their cups. 'What do you think?' Wright asked.

He hesitated before he answered. 'I don't know. It doesn't seem like a runaway, but then what? Let's hope it's not a kidnapping.'

They walked back to Watson's desk.

'How did the family seem?' Wright asked.

'Marcus, the boyfriend, didn't say too much. He provided us with the photo of Alison. The father is a different beast. Throwing his weight around. I don't think he appreciated having been called away from work. Imagine that, when your daughter is missing. And he was drinking — heavily.'

'What kind of work does he do?'

Watson shrugged. 'He owns a company. That's all I know, haven't had time to check him out. I'll do that right now, ma'am.'

Wright smiled and made her way back to her office.

The Companies House website came up with 14,000 hits on David Grant's name. Watson huffed and took his phone out of his pocket. He texted Sharon Walsh.

What does David do for a living?

Watson found a space in the almost full car park of the Royal Oak in South Meadows. He should have known, he thought, lunchtime. He surveyed the car park until he spotted the car he'd been looking for.

Entering through the door, he glanced at the clientele before approaching the bar. The Royal Oak prided itself on being a traditional public house in the area, which meant an individual interior, no large flatscreen TV on the walls, no radio on the sports channel, and a menu based on fresh food from local markets. Even the drinks were locally brewed.

After ordering half a pint of bitter, he walked into the restaurant.

'Thought you wouldn't turn up,' Monteith said, sipping his pint.

'Busy morning,' Watson replied as he sat down.

'I heard on the radio before I left. Missing young woman; body found buried and the usual nutters trying to ruin things for the rest of us.'

'All in a day's work, you should know that. Or have you lost your mojo since leaving?' Watson commented, while glancing at the menu.

'I wish I was still doing it instead of looking at banks of screens every night, thanks to Matthews and the Russells.' Monteith started pulling apart a beer mat. 'Has some fringe benefits though. Some nice ladies I can look at every night. Look, but don't touch.' Monteith raised his eyebrows and grinned.

Watson tried to stifle a laugh but failed. 'Typical!'

'Well looking at them is better than looking at the bald and flabby men or the flash kids losing their money faster than a Lewis Hamilton lap record around Silverstone. I've been there and got a lot of T-shirts, remember?'

One of the restaurant staff, who looked like she should still have been in school, wandered over to see if they were ready to order. Watson asked for a BLT baguette with salad. Monteith ordered the same with chips.

'How are the brothers?' Watson asked after the waiter had moved on.

'Keeping their powder dry at the moment. Nothing stands out. They are behaving themselves or keeping things quiet until they decide I'm not a threat. Their last chief of security, the one who left suddenly, his name's Tommy Burke. Lex, one of Jimmy's bodyguards, told me.'

'I'll check him out and get back to you,' Watson replied, making a note.

Over lunch, they caught up with each other. Monteith shared his concerns about Katie and how she was about to file for divorce.

'That was a wonderful meal,' Watson exclaimed. He called the waiter to pay the bill. 'I enjoyed that.'

They walked out and went into the car park. Watson's phone pinged. He looked at the message and smiled.

'Sally sending you dirty texts again?,' Monteith laughed while trying to locate his car keys.

'I wish,' Watson replied. 'No, that was the family liaison officer who is taking care of the missing girl's parents. She's just given me the name of the firm the dad, David Grant, works for. Argent Logistics.'

'Argent Logistics?' Monteith turned around.

'Yes, you heard of them?'

'I saw Allan carrying a file with that name on it into Jimmy's office the other day.'

CHAPTER SIX

Tuesday 3:23 a.m.

WATSON WAS CROUCHED BEHIND a car in the city's multi-storey. He watched the killer move, get up, and raise his gun. Shooting. A body tumbled. He panicked. I need to stop this. Why didn't I? Where did the gun come from? Where was it? NO. STOP, DON'T SHOOT.

'Terry, Terry wake up.' Sally was shaking him.

'What.' Watson shot up.

'It's ok, darling. You were shouting, "Don't shoot".' Sally stroked his head and back. 'You had that nightmare again.'

Watson looked around the dark bedroom, only illuminated by the streetlight peeping in through the curtains. He wiped the sweat from his face, threw the bedclothes back and peeled himself off the sodden sheet, swilling his face with cold water in the bathroom.

Sally followed him. 'Anything I can do?' She slid her arms around him from behind.

Watson dried his face and turned to face her, still in her embrace, kissing her on the lips.

'Thank you, but no. I have to work this out for myself.'

'Have you made that appointment with the police counsellor?'

'Don't you start,' he grumbled. 'The boss was on about seeing them yesterday morning.' He got out of her embrace and padded across the landing back to their bedroom.

'And she is right. Counselling could help you. At least think about it,' Sally pleaded.

Silently, he laid back with his arm covering his eyes, hoping to block out the night. Not wanting to fall asleep again in case the nightmare came back. He felt Sally move across, laying her face on his chest, her hand rubbing his head. He looked down at her.

'For me and the kids?'

'I'll think about it.'

Watson pulled into the only parking space available behind the Ravenswood City Hospital. He rubbed his eyes; the lack of sleep was catching up on him. Better be ready for the post-mortem, he thought grimly as he got out of the car and walked towards the morgue.

Mac's signature music hit his eardrums as soon as he opened the door. AC/DC's "Dirty Deeds Done Dirt Cheap" ramped up full blast. Mac was getting his tools ready when he looked up and saw Watson. He turned the music down.

'You must have titanium eardrums,' Watson joked.

'Heavy metal must be played loud. The louder the better.'

'It's okay in a large venue or an outdoor festival, but in here? Jesus, it's enough to give you brain damage, never mind hearing loss.'

Mac grinned. 'Did you know that on 15 July 2009, in Canada, Kiss achieved 136 decibels during their live performance? After noise complaints from neighbours in the area, the band was forced to turn the volume down.'

'Judging from the noise I heard coming in, it's a wonder some of your guests don't complain, and they're dead.'

Both burst out laughing. Mac's assistant came in. 'Our guest is ready for you, Mac.'

Mac directed Watson to the vantage room overlooking the morgue.

'You can ask questions through the intercom as we go along.'

Mac and his assistant started peeling back the carpet and black sheeting covering the body, being careful not to lose anything of significance and recording everything by taking pictures and audio-reporting their findings. Watson kept his questions to a minimum as he watched, fascinated by Mac's work.

'We're dealing with a female body here, Terry,' Mac said. 'She's five foot seven and about twenty-five to thirty. Cause of death is blunt force trauma to the back of the head.'

Watson scribbled the information down. 'Any other information? And I hate to ask but...' he hesitated.

Mac looked up at him. He nodded, 'Thank God no, she wasn't raped.'

Both men were relieved.

Mac continued, 'She was a blonde but not a natural one. I'd say she's been in the ground for say six months. Oh, and she was wearing a red tracksuit with a black top underneath when she died. Trainers size six. There's a tattoo of a swallow on her left shoulder, hopefully that will give you something to identify her by. Her arms and legs have cuts and bruises and the wrists and ankles show marks as if she'd been restrained.'

Watson sighed. *Poor girl.*

———

A black Range Rover Evoque with private number plates crawled through the city centre. The driver had picked its passenger up from a large waterside home. A four-bedroom, detached house with manicured lawns leading down to the river. The front was electrically gated with high walls. The house was a long way from the terraced, two up-two down council house on the Thelwell Estate that the owner had grown up in.

The driver turned the Range Rover into the car park at the back of the council offices, parking up close to the main doors. They weren't going to stay long.

Getting out, he went round to the back of the car and opened the rear passenger door. Jimmy Russell got out, straightening his suit jacket and tie. He nodded to Ray, the driver, and after locking the car, both strode purposefully into the council building.

In the foyer, a smart-looking woman wearing a lanyard passed them. As she did, a note changed hands. Jimmy looked at it, nodded, and turned around. He stormed out back to his car.

Tuesday 11 a.m.

Monteith was talking to the security guards and floorwalkers in the casino's bar. Jimmy Russell had thrown him into the deep and

Monteith knew he was being watched. *I don't want to end up like the previous head of security.* Besides, he had his family to think of.

The sight of Ray struggling to keep up with Jimmy as they flew past him and up to the offices caught his eye. He observed them, but didn't spring into action. *Best to carry on.* He'd soon enough find out what had happened. Both Ray and Lex, slowly at first, were beginning to trust him with some of the ongoings within the Russell Empire. Not the big stuff. They were not stupid.

In his office, Jimmy grabbed a drink and flung himself onto the leather sofa.

'I take it didn't go in our favour?' Allan commented from a large armchair.

'You got that right. It's been pushed to a subcommittee. The police want more information on it. Said they were not happy at a licence being granted.'

'I thought Spedding said it would pass easily?'

'Well, he was wrong!' Jimmy yelled, hatred in his voice. He got up and started to pace up and down the office ringing his hands. 'That jerk is starting to really piss me off.'

'Everybody seems to be pissing you off lately.'

'What's that mean?' Jimmy turned to face Allan.

'Just that. You're snapping at people for the smallest of things. You had a go at Lex the other day because he spilled something on your precious carpet.'

'So what? He should be careful!' Jimmy sat back down on the armchair next to Allan. 'Funny isn't it? You have always tried to keep me in check when I go off on one. You are my conscience, my dear brother, and I am grateful for that. God knows where I would be without you.'

'So, what do you want to do with Spedding?' Allan asked.

Jimmy frowned. 'I think we need to pay him a little visit. Remind him of his obligations.'

Allan nodded. 'Good thinking, brother.'

Monteith was walking towards the lift as Ray exited one of them, looking frazzled.

'What's up with the boss?'

'Tonight's going to be tough,' Ray replied.

Monteith looked at him questioningly.

'When things don't go right for the boss, then everyone gets it, even when it's not your fault,' Ray explained.

As they walked between the open double doors leading to the kitchen, Lex appeared, munching on an apple. 'Well?'

'He's up there having a go at Allan,' Ray replied.

'Brilliant,' Lex sighed, throwing the apple core in a nearby bin. 'Hopefully Allan can calm him down'.

'Does this happen often?' Monteith asked.

Lex looked at Ray as if seeking his approval to speak to an ex-copper before responding. 'No, it does not happen too often,' he replied, finally. 'You saw the plans for a gentleman's private club on one of your last visits before you joined us?'

He nodded. 'I vaguely remember. Why?'

Ray poured himself a coffee. 'Well, there seems to be one obstacle which is proving hard to remove. And when the boss is not happy, everyone suffers.'

Monteith shook his head. 'Thanks for the heads-up. I will stay looking at my screens tonight. If you want somewhere to hide, you know where to come.' He could see Lex giving him the evil eye.

'Right, I've got work to do,' Lex announced, signalling with his fingers "I'm watching you" before disappearing.

Monteith turned to Ray. 'What did I do or say to upset him?'

Ray laughed. 'It's not personal. He hates all police, past and present.'

They both walked into the casino. 'Story goes that his dad was a leading detective in the big smoke somewhere. He took his life after accusations of being involved in a police protection racket. He denied it but was found guilty. They found him hanging in his cell six months into his sentence. He was still pleading his innocence. Alex doted on his dad and went off the rails after. He served five years for GBH on a policeman. After coming out, he moved here and started working for the Russells.'

Before he could ask about Ray's background, the lift doors opened, and the Russell brothers stepped out.

Allan signalled to Ray.

'Looks like I am required. No rest for the wicked.' Putting down his cup, Ray followed his bosses.

'Wicked is right,' Monteith murmured.

Watson sat at his desk. Being Detective Chief Inspector brought with it an office. An office he did not feel comfortable in even after eighteen months on the position. Although his office was next to the DSI's and he could see out into the main room, he still wanted to be out there with his fellow officers. He preferred being on the front line, and loved it, chasing the criminals. Paperwork was a necessary evil in the police force, and that was what he was in the middle of doing.

Lorimer stuck his head around the office door while putting his jacket on. He could see French also rushing to get out.

'Got a sighting of our couple of fraudsters,' Lorimer said. 'Shopping centre at the Meadows. Security is keeping tabs on them until we arrive.'

'Good, you and French take charge. Don't take nothing for granted with the supermarket security.'

'Gotcha gov, will keep you updated.'

Taking his coffee cup, Watson went across to the information boards holding the latest information of the ongoing investigations. Mac's report and photos from the post-mortem of the buried body had been sent through. As he put the new information up, DSI Wright came to stand beside him.

'There are still no sightings of Alison Grant. Mr Grant gave PC Sharon Walsh her orders to leave last night. Something about upsetting his wife, which I don't believe from what she told me. He is just a control freak. I think I will try to speak to the boyfriend, Marcus, again. He might open up away from her parents.'

'Within reason, don't go looking for trouble,' Wright warned.

'Me? Trouble? Never.'

'What about the body from the building estate?' Wright asked.

'No missing persons matching the description,' he added.

Wright looked closer at the photo of the swallow tattoo. 'Interesting tattoo, pity it's so degraded'.

'Oh, why?'

'Tattooists use different types of ink. The cheaper the ink the more it fades. Also, it depends on the way it is applied, either by a tattoo gun or tattoo pen.'

'And you know this because...'

'I did have a life before the police, DCI Watson.'

———

As agreed, DS Lorimer and DC French parked their car in the employees' car park at the back of the Meadows Shopping Centre. The Head of Security was waiting by the entrance to escort them into the CCTV room. A bank of thirty screens filled one wall, giving the operators a view to both entrances of the shopping centre, the main concourse, and the front of each shop. There were also a few covering the insides of the high street supermarket.

'Where are they?' Lorimer asked.

'There.' The CCTV operator zoomed in to offer them a close-up of the pair sitting on a bench. The couple didn't stand out from the rest of the shoppers.

'Have they bought anything?' French asked.

'Only drinks and something to eat, and they paid that in cash. We checked,' the security guard said.

'Looks like we have movement', the operator said, pointing at the screen. The couple were now walking into the supermarket, which dominated the shopping centre.

'How do you want to play this?' the security guard asked.

'We cannot arrest them until they have paid for goods by a stolen debit card. Keep your distance till then. DC French and I are going to do a bit of shopping.'

'Are you buying dinner for tonight?' French suggested.

'Yes, if you want. As long as it is two credit card fraudsters, well done!'

'I couldn't eat a whole one. Anyway, I'm a vegetarian,' French chuckled.

Don Spedding exited the council offices and walked across to his car. A black Range Rover Evoke was parked next to his. Leaning on it was Ray. He smirked and Don froze. He turned to come face to face with Allan Russell.

'I hope you were not thinking of doing a runner, Don. That wouldn't be very friendly.'

Allan put a hand on Don's shoulder. 'My brother would like a quick chat with you.'

Ray opened the back door of the Range Rover.

'Get in,' Jimmy Russell snapped.

Don tentatively stepped up and slid across the leather seat next to Jimmy. Allan got in after him. Ray closed the door, staying outside.

Jimmy scrutinised Don. 'What happened?'

Don shivered. He opened his mouth and swallowed. 'Sorry, Mr Russell. I could not stop it from being referred to the subcommittee. The majority went with the police's concerns over licencing and wanted to investigate the proposal closer. I fought for you to get it through, but...'

Russell put his hand up. 'I have had enough of your whining. You make sure it gets through next time. Do you understand?' He looked at Don, murder in his eyes.

'I will try my best, but it won't be easy,' Don squeaked.

Allan reached forward into the pocket behind the driver's seat and pulled out a large envelope, handing it to Don. 'I don't think your wife would be happy seeing these.'

With shaking hands, Don opened the envelope. He paled. 'You cannot do that. Those photos... we... my secretary... how did you get into my office?'

Jimmy grinned. 'We did a pretty good job, right? In flagrante, I think is what they call it. So I take it we are clear?'

Don avoided his look. He nodded.

'NOW GET OUT.'

CHAPTER SEVEN

CLOSE TO THE END of the school day, Watson parked his car outside St Mary's sixth form school and got out. Parents in oversized cars, trying to get as close to the gates as they could for their precious kids not to have to walk so far, were causing traffic to build up. *Cars on steroids*, he thought. *Too big for city roads.* The designers must have a field day trying to come up with the biggest one that they could. Over the last few weeks, he and Sally had been mulling over changing her Citroen Picasso, or the bus, as the kids called it, for something smaller.

The bell rang, and a swarm of teens came flying out of the school. It was not long before he spotted Marcus crossing the road just down from where he was standing with a group of his friends. 'Marcus,' he called as he moved towards the group, gracing them with a flash of his ID card.

'Chief Inspector, have you found her?' Marcus was quick to ask.

'No, not yet. You haven't heard from her either, I take it?'

'No. We're going out again to look for her this evening,' Marcus added, his five friends nodding along.

Watson continued. "I asked you last time we met if there was any trouble at her home. You said no. Is that still right?"

'You should talk to that trainer at the athletics club, Ian Fellows. Creepy,' one of the young women shouted.

'Steph, shush.' Marcus shot her a look.

'What about it, Marcus? What's with the athletics trainer?'

Marcus shrugged. 'You and your big mouth, Steph. Yeah, Alison's coach was being a bit overly friendly with her and a few of the others. Alison told me that there was nothing to it and that we should stop worrying, but his behaviour made me uncomfortable.'

'What did he do?'

'He would take them out for extra training. The county trials are coming up, so he said. Alison and the others needed the training to give them the boost for the trials.'

'That's it?'

'Yeah, nothing to it.' Marcus walked back to the car with Watson. "You won't tell her dad about this? You've seen what he's like, jumping at everyone.'

'I can't promise anything, but if this coach Ian Fellows had anything to do with Alison's disappearance, he will have to be told.'

Watson said goodbye, walked towards his car, got in and drove off.

Watson exited the lift and walked into the office. He noticed the others gathered around Lorimer and French.

'What did I miss?' He looked at Lorimer whose hair, face, jacket and top were covered in a lovely colour purple. 'What the hell happened to you?'

'Beetroot.'

'Pardon?'

'Beetroot. I am covered in beetroot juice.'

'I hate to ask why?' Watson grinned as he sat on the edge of a desk. 'This better be a good story.'

'Those credit card fraudsters did not come in peacefully. Well, one of them didn't. We had him down an aisle when he picked up a large jar of beetroot and chucked it at us. It smashed against part of the racking, covering me and one of the security guards.'

French, trying to keep a straight face, continued the tale, 'We managed to catch him when he rounded the end of another aisle straight into an abandoned trolley. They are both in the cells downstairs. We will interview them later when the duty solicitor arrives.'

Watson burst out laughing. 'You had better hope none of that was filmed and ends up on Facebook or YouTube.'

French turned to Lorimer. 'Come on, beetroot juice, you had better get yourself cleaned up before the interview.'

As the two of them left the office, Watson made his way over to the information board and put Ian Fellows' name and a question mark against Alison Grant's disappearance.

'Someone we know?' DSI Wright joined him.

'Spoke to the boyfriend, Marcus, and some of Alison's friends. Fellows came up in conversation. He's Alison's coach at the athletics club. They said he was giving a little more attention to Alison and some of the other young women at the club.'

Looking at a photograph of the body from the industrial estate on the board, he asked, 'Any of the local tattooists recognise their handiwork?'

'No luck there,' Sandall replied. 'Swallows are common, apparently. Oh, and Mac rang with an update. He has sent X-rays and impressions to the local dentists.'

'Hopefully, we will get a hit,' Watson said. He grabbed a cup of coffee and stopped off at Sandall's desk. 'Paul, can you look for details on this Ian Fellows? Check how long he has been a coach and how long he has been in Ravenswood.'

'On it, sir.'

Twenty minutes later, Sandall knocked on Watson's door. 'Sir?'

'Yes, come in. Is it about Ian Fellows?'

Sandall sat down. 'When I was checking HOLMES, his name was flagged up.'

'In connection to what?' Watson asked.

'The county force is interested in him.' Sandall passed over the details. 'Looks like they have an ongoing investigation. That's who to contact.'

Watson read the details. 'Jeff Johnson, I know him. Thanks Paul, I'll give him a ring. Good work.'

Tuesday Evening

In his office, Monteith was skimming the screens in front of him. The casino was quiet, it being the beginning of the week. Most of the money was made from Thursday up to the weekend, when the high rollers came to play. The restaurant and bar helped cover the cost of keeping the doors open for the rest of the week. Waitresses mingled with customers playing the fruit machines, serving drinks and bar snacks to the gullible and desperate, hoping to win the big jackpot. At the big tables, drinks were served, but food was not allowed. The restaurant had a good reputation because the Russells employed top chefs; only a select few could afford to book a table.

How many of them did the Russells have in their pocket? Monteith mused as he tucked into his chicken and chips, which he washed down with a bottle of still water.

He heard the security pad for the door of the office being used before Allan Russell entered.

'Everything okay?' Allan asked, as he walked towards Monteith.

'Yep,' he replied between mouthfuls. 'Has your brother calmed down?'

'Yes, he has,' Allan replied. 'How did you know?'

'I saw him come back this afternoon looking furious. Ray mentioned something about keeping out of his way tonight.'

'Yes, he's alright. Just something that needed sorting.'

Monteith's eye was drawn towards the screen. A smartly dressed man who had been playing the jackpot machines for quite some time, grabbed a waitress and yelled at her. She hollered for support, and within seconds, two security guards appeared. Monteith and Allan Russell watched as the guards grabbed the man and dragged him towards the entrance to throw him out.

Then down by the toilets, a young lad in a denim jacket and red baseball cap appeared to be checking the place out as if planning to do something in the ruckus. Monteith zoomed a camera onto the lad.

Allan spotted him too and was on the radio in seconds, requesting the security guards to get down there.

Monteith and Allan saw the lad pass a small package to another lad going into the toilet. Quickly followed by another package to a lady exiting the women's.

'The cheeky bastard,' Allan exclaimed.

'Or he's got a death wish,' Monteith murmured as Allan flew out of the room.

He watched what was unfolding on the screens. Three security guards converged on the unsuspecting lad just as he was doing another deal. Seeing the guards, the lad tried to make his escape, but to no avail. Around the corner was Lex who had the lad in an arm lock. Monteith saw Allan approach, striding slowly and deliberately. He looked grim.

I would not want to be in the lad's shoes. Monteith shivered. He continued watching, unable to avert his eyes. The lad was clearly in pain, held tightly by Lex. Allan seemed to ask him questions and from what Monteith could see, wasn't too pleased with the answers. The lad was squirming and then emptied his pockets. Monteith thought he saw a stack of cash and small bags — pills maybe? He saw Allan signalling to hand it over, then Lex and two guards taking the lad away towards the rear exit.

Monteith was puzzled. *Why they were taking the lad out of the back?* Switching between CCTV cameras, he picked them up as they came out into the floodlit backyard. He watched the guards holding the lad as Lex approached. He noticed Lex had the bags of drugs in his hand and was opening them. The lad was fighting hard to break away, but failing. Lex walked up to the lad and forced the drugs down his throat.

The office door opened. Quickly, Monteith turned his attention to the monitor focused on the casino floor, but not fast enough.

Allan strode into the room. 'You watched?'

'I will keep an eye out in case he turns up again,' Monteith said, his heart beating a little faster.

'No need. I hate drugs and people like Wayne Marsh who think it's all right to sell drugs in my establishment. He won't be coming back.' With a cold smile, Allan turned and left the office.

'I bet he won't,' Monteith mumbled.

CHAPTER EIGHT

Wednesday Morning

DSI WRIGHT SAT BEHIND her desk, looking out over the main office. A career officer, she had forgone raising a family to concentrate on getting as high as she could in the force. Now in her mid-forties, she was well on her way.

Before her, she could see a group of talented officers who would back each other to the ends of the earth. DCI Terry Watson and DS Keith Monteith were close friends and newly promoted DS Karl Lorimer, another strong member of the team, was beginning to forge a partnership with DC Emma French. Last but not least was DC Paul Sandall. Slowly getting his feet under the table, he was an expert at collecting and assessing data to support investigations.

As long as she could keep Matthews from sticking his nose in too much, she was certain this team would grow from strength to strength.

Picking up her notes and her mug of coffee, she strolled into the main office and stood next to Watson at the board.

He started the brief, 'Right ladies and gentlemen, let's get this briefing going. Karl and Emma, where are we?'

Emma stood up. 'The pair were interviewed and charged last night with five counts of debit card fraud. They are due in court this afternoon.'

'Excellent! Not all our work is high profile and makes the front pages, but it is as important for our community.' She smiled.

'Amen.' Everyone joined in before breaking out in laughter. This was the type of thing Wright liked about the team, the togetherness and humour.

'DCI Watson, any update on Alison Grant?'

'Nothing. Sharon Walsh, the family liaison officer, is due to visit Mrs Grant this morning. I met Alison's boyfriend Marcus yesterday and he and their friends were going to search again after school; I've not heard back from him yet. They gave us the name of Ian Fellows. He was Alison's athletics coach, and they said he took too much interest in some of the girls on the team. Alison being one.'

'Tread carefully with this. She might still show up and we don't want to point fingers when there's no need,' Wright said.

'I'm waiting to hear back from DI Jeff Johnson from county. I rang yesterday and left him a message. They are interested in Fellows.'

A phone went off. DC Sandall picked it up.

Watson continued, 'And the body found at the building site. None of the dentists Mac contacted has been in touch.'

'Boss?' DC Sandall said. 'That was control. Railway maintenance this morning found a body of a girl in the bushes on an embankment. She was wearing a tracksuit.'

Sharon Walsh parked her Mini Countryman outside the Grants' house. She had been waiting for David to leave for work before approaching the property, not wanting to bump into him again.

She walked up the driveway and pressed the doorbell. Joan opened it, face tear-stained, still wearing a dressing gown.

'Mrs Grant, are you okay?'

Joan nodded, opened the door, and made her way back into the front room. Sharon closed the door behind her and entered the living room.

'Mrs Grant?'

'Have you found her?' Joan looked tired and drawn.

'No, I'm sorry.' Sharon sat on the edge of a chair facing Joan.

'I thought that's why you came round,' Joan uttered, shoulders sagging.

'I came to see how you, your husband and Alex were doing, and also to see if you had heard from her.'

Joan shook her head. 'No. Marcus came over last night, said he and a few of their friends were going out looking again, but they didn't find her.'

'Listen, Joan, why don't you get yourself changed, and I will make us a coffee,' Sharon smiled.

Joan nodded and made her way towards the stairs. 'Thank you.'

Sharon put the kettle on then, hearing the shower running, she took the opportunity to look around the living room. Photos of family holidays, seemingly taken years ago. The obligatory school year photos with both Alison and Alex sitting proud and grinning like Cheshire cats. Some ornaments.

Hearing the shower being switched off, she turned to the kitchen and made the drinks.

'That's better,' Joan said, as she entered the kitchen.

'Just looking at your garden — very nice,' Sharon commented, handing a mug of tea to Joan.

'Thank you. I am the green-fingered one. David is always busy with work. If he's not at the office, he is away at some meeting.' Joan sat down at the kitchen table, cupping the mug in her hands, not looking up.

'Is he away often?' Sharon was leaning against the sink.

'At least two weeks a month. He's been working hard to keep the business going.'

'That's Argent Logistics? I remember you saying last time I was here.'

Joan nodded. 'It's been tough over the last year. I don't know much about it, but the snippets of phone calls David gets even during the evening suggest things are not going well. Possible takeover, I heard him say once.'

'When we were here last time, your husband seemed...' she paused, 'hostile, angry even.'

'I think the wording you need is, he was being an arsehole,' Joan said. 'I rang him at work, which pissed him off. When he got home, we had a blazing row. He was just about to go into a big important meeting with a client and I had probably ruined any chance of a deal.' Joan tensed up.

'Wasn't he at all worried about Alison going missing?'

'No, not David. He dismissed my concern; said she would come home when she was ready. He only has time for his precious job. Has been like that for the last year.'

She could see the dam Joan built to contain her feelings was about to burst. 'Before the last twelve months was he –'

'A normal husband and father?' Joan finished her sentence. 'Yes. He was very supportive of Alison and Alex in all they did. We used to watch Alison running and Alex playing rugby for their schools at the weekend. We went on family holidays. But now, he hardly has time for us. It's all work, work, work. I used to talk to him about it, but now I have given up. It always ends up in him storming out.'

Sharon moved and sat down at the table opposite Joan.

'Joan, can we talk about Alison?' Sharon asked quietly.

'Umm,' Joan glanced up. She nodded.

'How was Alison before she disappeared? Was she worried about anything?'

Joan thought. 'No, she was her normal self. Concentrating on training, running the half-marathon to raise money for breast cancer. Her aunt, my sister, died six months ago from it. I think she had close to a thousand pounds in sponsorship.'

'I'm sorry about your sister.'

'The end was a bit of a blessing; she was in a lot of pain.'

Sharon took a deep breath. 'I'm sorry to ask but, may I have a look at Alison's room, please?'

'Why?' Joan looked confused.

'I have been tasked with collecting something that has Alison's DNA on it, like a hairbrush or toothbrush. It's so we have something on record if we get a lead on her whereabouts. We would have asked before now, but because David was...'

Joan didn't ask questions but took Sharon upstairs. It was not a typical girl's room; Alison seemed more of a tomboy. On a wall were posters of Paula Radcliffe, Jo Pavey, and Lisa Dobriskey. Tracksuits were hanging on the outside of her wardrobe. A photo of Marcus and one of the two of them in an embrace stood on her night stand.

Sharon donned gloves and took the hairbrush from the dressing table, putting it in an evidence bag. She walked out of Alison's bedroom and nodded to Joan. 'Thank you.'

As they re-entered the living room, Sharon's phone rang. She moved to the front window to answer it. It was a short call. She turned around and her expression was one of pain.

Joan started to cry.

Police tape decorated the area, flapping away in the wind. It ran for fifty metres alongside the road beside the railway embankment. The road had been blocked off at either end, the traffic diverted through a nearby village. The railway line had also been closed, which caused even more disruption to the already angry commuters.

Police vehicles, CSI vans, and Mac's morgue bus filled the road. On the grassy verge of the track, the British rail maintenance workers were giving their statements to a couple of police officers. CSI were searching along the curb-side embankment.

DCI Watson parked his car behind a police car. He was with Paul Sandall; Wright had told Watson to get him a bit more involved, and out of the office. They stood at the top of the embankment, looking down to the thick hawthorn bushes and long grass where the body of the woman had been found.

Mac and the CSI team had managed to erect a tent over the body within the slope of the bushes. Watson and Sandall signed in with a PC and walked over towards Mac.

'Okay to come in?' Watson asked.

'Yes, but be careful. It's a bit tight in here.' Mac stuck his head out, level with Watson's knees. 'One at a time, I think.' With that, he disappeared.

Watson went in first, bending to get in. He looked at the body and sighed.

'Looks like you know who this is?' Mac looked up.

'Alison Grant,' Watson replied. 'She went missing on Monday while out for a run. The family gave us a description of the clothing she's wearing.' He added, looking at the lifeless body of the young woman, still wearing her tracksuit and trainers, 'That's her alright. How did she die?'

'Hit on the back of the head here.' Mac pointed to his crown. 'Been tied up at some point. There are abrasions on her wrists and ankles. I will get a better view back at the morgue.'

'Was she killed here or elsewhere and brought here?'

'Elsewhere, then dumped. The wound at the back of her head is a couple of days old, by the look of it. And there is no blood spatter on anything surrounding her.'

'Do you have a time of death?' Watson's knees were clicking as he got up.

'Possibly twelve to eighteen hours. Rigor had set in, but it's releasing its grip. I will have a better timescale later.'

'Thanks, Mac. Can Paul have a quick look? He's new and I want him to get up to speed on this.'

'Ooh, a newbie. Not had one of those in the morgue for a long time,' Mac smiled. 'Please show him in.'

Watson exited the tent, pulling his gloves off as he went. He looked at Sandall and nodded. 'Yes, it's Alison Grant all right. Go and see. Mac is waiting for you.'

Sandall made his way over to the tent. Watson took a big breath and slowly exhaled. It was bad enough seeing dead bodies, but children... something nobody should see or get used to.

Surveying the area, he spotted a uniformed officer leaving the maintenance workers who had begun to pack up and move off. He recognised him as PC Gary Barnes, from his initial visit to the Grant residence.

'Good to see you again, sir.' Barnes puffed out his cheeks.

'And you, PC Barnes. How did the maintenance workers find her?'

'They were checking the lines for faults and clearing up the line and surrounding area of rubbish, which can be a hazard to trains. One of them nipped behind a bush to take a leak. He found her on his way back. Almost fell over her due to the dark. They rang the yard who contacted us.'

'So, she was likely left here sometime yesterday evening or early this morning?'

'Looks like it,' Barnes confirmed.

Mac and Sandall emerged from the tent. Sandall white as a sheet.

'How long before you are ready to take Alison back to the morgue?' Watson asked.

'About half an hour, just a few things to check over and we will be finished.' Mac was taking his gloves off and wiping his forehead.

'I would have come over anyway to check on an update on the other body, to see if you had an ID.'

'Nothing last night, but I haven't checked my emails this morning. Come by later and I'll know, and I'll have laid Alison out for the post-mortem.'

'Mr and Mrs Grant will come for the identification,' Watson reminded Mac.

'Yes, I can get that arranged prior to the post-mortem.' With that, Mac walked off.

Watson turned to Sandall and Barnes. 'Right, Gary, can you get back to the station and write out the statements from the maintenance men? Give DCI Wright a copy, please.'

'Yes sir, anything else?' Barnes asked.

'No, but make sure your boss knows you've been helping us. I will let DSI Wright know when I get back.'

'Paul, that leaves you and I. We're going to the Grants' home. I'll let Sharon know we're on the way,' Watson said as he took out his phone.

———

Sharon had brought Joan into the viewing gallery. Watson and Sandall stood beside them. By the time they arrived at the Grants, Joan Grant was in hysterics. She had been trying to get hold of her husband, to no avail. Lorimer and French had been sent over to his workplace to fetch him.

The curtains opened up, covering the glass. Joan shivered, then screamed Alison's name and started sobbing uncontrollably. She wavered and then collapsed on the floor. Sharon knelt down and hugged her.

Watson walked into Mac's office five minutes later. 'It never gets easier.' He slumped onto a battered chair in the corner.

'Nope, and I have seen it all. Where is the mother?' Mac poured them a mug of coffee.

'Sharon and Paul have taken her to the comfort room.'

Mac handed a mug to Watson. 'Is the father around?'

'Work. Keith and Emma have gone to find him.'

'You should keep an eye on Paul. Very interested in pathology. Asking all the right questions.'

'We will send him to all autopsies from now on,' Watson said.

'Just because you and Keith got squeamish with that bloater the other month.'

'That was Keith, I was alright.' Watson pleaded innocence.

'Yer right, which was why you were over the other side of the room for most of it.'

'At least I stayed in the room, Keith was so green I had to send him home.' Both broke into laughter, which they immediately stifled. Not when Mrs Grant was close by. Sandall stuck his head around the door.

'Sharon's taking Mrs Grant home. Mr Grant still hasn't arrived.'

'Good. Mac is it alright for Paul to stay for Alison's post mortem?' Watson winked at Mac.

'Me?' Paul exclaimed.

'Yes, is that okay? Mac said you were very interested earlier on.'

'I would love to. If I wasn't a detective, I would have tried the medical profession.'

'See, he would an all,' Mac laughed.

'Can't I?' Sandall asked.

'Yes, why not. You can join me. Gives you some experience.'

Mac, grinning, searched his desk and pulled out a file. 'Got sent an email from a local dentist.' He handed the file to Watson. 'The body. Her name is Claire Townsend. Her dentist last saw her three months ago.'

'Thanks, Mac. We can compare her stats to missing persons now we know she lived in the city.'

As they left the office, another gurney was being brought in by Mac's assistant. He handed Mac the paperwork.

'Who have we here? Ah, the teenager found in the park this morning. Suspected drug overdose. On his person was identification for a Wayne Marsh. Welcome to my humble abode, Wayne. We'll make you comfortable, then we will talk later.'

Sandall nudged Watson. 'Gov, does he always talk to them?'

'Yep, and also sometimes sings to them.'

Watson arrived back at headquarters by mid-afternoon. By three p. m., the whiteboards had been updated with all the new information.

He stood in front of the boards waiting for the remaining seats to be taken by uniformed officers who had been seconded to him for the duration of the search, PC Gary Barnes included. The room was filled with the sound of scraping chairs, and chatter.

'Ladies and gentlemen, could I have your attention please.' He pointed to a photograph of Alison. 'Alison went missing on Monday morning while on a training run. She was found this morning on a railway embankment to the north of the city. We need to identify the people we haven't spoken to on her usual routes. Did any of them see anything that morning? Also, check with those we have spoken to if they can remember anything else.' He pointed at a map with Alison's routes marked out.

Turning around, Watson asked Lorimer, 'Karl what's the update on Alison's father? Have we heard from him yet?'

'Emma and I went to Argent Logistics where Mr Grant works. His PA said he had gone to see a client out of the city. She tried to get hold of him, but his phone kept going to voicemail. She said she would contact us if she managed to get through.'

'Thanks, Karl. Is Sharon still at the Grants' house?'

'I believe so, boss.'

'Good, so if he turns up there we are covered. Right, next to the boyfriend, Marcus Devonport. I spoke to him yesterday,' Watson sat on the edge of a desk. 'He seemed genuinely upset at Alison's disappearance. He's been nothing short of helpful and engaging and has been actively searching for her.'

'Where have we got with this Ian Fellows fella?' DSI Wright asked.

'One of Alison's friends,' Watson looked at his notes, "Steph, mentioned his name. Marcus told her to shut up when she said his name. DI Jeff Johnson from county informed me they have an ongoing investigation, ORACLE. Ian Fellows, it turns out is on their radar. According to Jeff, Fellows wasn't in Ravenswood the morning of Alison's disappearance. He was at work in the south of the county. They have him under close surveillance. DC Sandall has updated HOLMES with all the details.

'So, we can definitely rule him out,' Wright said.

'Sounds like he is a lot of things, but not a murderer.'

'I want you to interview Marcus again, see what more he can come up with. And Steph, let's see what she knows,' said Wright.

Watson nodded and took a quick mouthful of coffee before continuing. 'Yes, ma'am. Then we have Claire Townsend.' He pointed at her photo on the board. 'Emma, you have the details?'

DC Emma French stood. 'Claire Townsend, age twenty-four, went missing three months ago. Her body was found buried at

Copeland industrial estate under the floor of one of the units. She was wrapped in carpet. I will be disclosing the news to her husband later today with a liaison officer.'

'Do we know who owned the unit prior to the developers moving in?'

'A national tyre, brakes and exhaust company. I'm awaiting a call from their HQ with the date of when they shut up shop and a list of employees that worked there.'

'Thank you, Emma. Can you and Karl go to speak to Claire Townsend's husband? Paul you come with me to pick up Marcus Devonport. Sergeant Makepeace, can you organise some of your officers to do another door to door around the routes Alison Grant may have taken, see if we can get any more information? Thank you, everyone.'

CHAPTER NINE

MONTEITH STOOD BY HIS car looking at his mother-in-law's house. He hadn't spoken to Katie, and he hadn't seen the kids since they'd left.

His boots felt heavy as he walked up to the front door and knocked. Waiting was agonising. He heard laughter from behind the door, kids' laughter. The door opened and Katie stood there.

'What do you want?' she spat.

'To talk, to explain, to see the kids.'

'We don't have anything to talk about. You have chosen your friends over us.'

'Believe me, there wasn't much of a choice.'

'Daddy!' Pixie screamed with delight, moving towards the door. He picked her up and hugged her close.

'When are we coming home?' Pixie asked.

He looked at his wife before answering. 'Mummy and daddy have to talk about working that out. That's why I'm here, and to see you and Rachael.'

Pixie looked at her mother who was quick to show a faint smile.

'Can I come in?' He knew she could not refuse him in front of their daughter. Katie stood back as he carried Pixie into the living room.

Once drinks were made and Rachael and Pixie had spent ten minutes with their daddy, Katie's mother took the girls into the garden.

They sat down opposite each other at the dining room table, from where they could see the kids playing in the back garden. He looked at Katie, who sat like she was judge and jury on what was left of their marriage.

'First, I want you to know that I love you and the kids, and being away from you all is tearing me apart.' He was cut short.

'Quit working for the Russells and find another security job. There are plenty out there,' replied Katie. It sounded like an ultimatum.

'I can't do that.' He shook his head.

'Well, then we have nothing more to say to each other.' Katie stood up.

'SIT DOWN!' He could not control himself. This was make or break time.

'What?' Katie's eyes flew wide open. She looked shocked.

'I said sit down,' he forced himself to speak calmly. 'I need you to know why I cannot do what you ask of me.'

Katie slowly sat back down. 'Terry, you're frightening me.'

'Just hear me out, and if you still feel the way you do then...' his voice faded. He took a swig of his coffee. 'I need you to promise, none of this goes outside these four walls, okay?'

She nodded.

'I cannot quit working for the Russells because I'm working for them as a undercover police officer. They have no idea I'm still on the force's payroll.'

Katie looked like she had been slapped across the face. 'But you quit the force?'

He shook his head. 'That was the story the bosses put out. Before the Russells abducted me, Chief Superintendent Matthews wanted me to get closer to the Russells to gather information so we can bring down their operation. Inside information.'

Katie went to speak, but he put his hand up. 'Let me continue, then if you have questions, I will try to answer them. Matthews threatened to put me back on the beat if I refused. Then the Russells abducted me and offered me a position. They threatened me. It was made quite clear that if I refused, your and the kids' lives would be in danger. They wanted me to head the security at their casino.'

Katie gasped and broke down in tears. He got up and tried to put his arms around her, but she shrugged him off. He reluctantly sat back down and continued, 'Then I woke up in hospital.'

Katie wiped her eyes and sat back, staring at her husband. 'What happened after you discharged yourself and went back to the station? Leaving me in the taxi not knowing what was happening or what was going on inside you?'

'When I told DSI Wright, she, Terry, and the others were gunning for us to arrest them for my abduction, but Matthews wanted me to take them up on their offer. It was that or I'd be out of a job, and you know how much my career means to me. I had the Russells threatening you and the kids on one hand. And I had Matthews' threat on the other. I had no choice. You have to believe me.'

Katie shivered. 'How long are you going to be working for the Russells? Weeks? Months?'

'Until we have enough on them to charge them with something that'll release their stranglehold on this city. I report to DSI Wright. If things get too hairy for me, then they will pull me out and arrest them.'

Katie got up and stared out of the window. Rachael and Pixie were playing chase with their grandmother. Laughter permeated through the glass. Monteith joined her.

'I want you to go now,' Katie said. 'I need to think things over. Think about what you have told me.'

'I understand. It's a lot to take in.' He went to kiss Katie, but she pulled her head away. He left her and went into the garden to say goodbye to the kids. Five minutes later, he started his car and drove off to the casino, glancing back just in time to notice the black Range Rover pulling out, following him.

'GET ME WHO IS IN CHARGE OF THIS PLACE,' David Grant boomed, standing in the middle of the reception area of the Ravenswood police headquarters. 'I WANT THEM DOWN HERE NOW!'

The duty officer behind the reception desk said composedly, 'Sir, I need you to calm down–'

'CALM DOWN? My daughter has been murdered and I only found out about it when I came home. I want to make a complaint. The incompetence of this place!' He slammed his fist on the desk.

The officer took a step back. 'Sir, calm down. You will not see someone in this condition. Let me take your name and I will enquire upstairs.'

'Tell them David Grant is here. NOW,' he bellowed.

———

Ten minutes later, DSI Wright, along with DC Sandall, appeared from the stairwell. Grant was pacing around like a caged animal.

'Mr Grant?' Wright approached with her hand out straight.

Grant looked at her. 'You in charge?' he snapped.

'Detective Superintendent Wright, and this is Detective Constable Sandall. Let me first tell me how sorry I am for your loss. Please, follow me and I'll update you on our investigation.' Wright oozed confidence and calmness.

Grant looked flustered, but followed her to an interview room. He stood against the back wall of the room. Wright and Sandall pulled out chairs and sat down at a floor-bolted table.

'Mr Grant, would you like to take a seat?' Wright said.

Grant leaned his hands on the desk. 'I came home to an inconsolable wife and one of your so-called "family liaison officers" to be told my daughter is dead. And nobody thought fit to contact me?'

'Mr Grant, sit down,' Wright ordered.

Grant whipped a chair away from the desk and sat on it. 'Satisfied?'

'Thank you. Now Mr Grant, when your wife identified Alison's body she told us you were at work. We sent detectives to your office, but you were out and your PA could not trace you. Your mobile went to voicemail, so we were unable to reach you.'

Grant opened his mouth as if to protest, but then closed it. 'Erm yes, I was in a meeting with a client.'

'And this client had no phones at their offices that your PA could ring?'

'Erm no, they have just set up. Anyway, what happened to Alison? Have you caught the bastard who killed her?'

'She was found on a railway embankment not far from where you live. Network rail maintenance workers discovered her this morning. And Mr Grant, I don't believe I said she was murdered.'

Grant's face went bright red with anger. 'DSI Wright, stop playing word games and find her murderer.'

'It's early in our enquiries and we have not had the post-mortem report back. Until we do, we don't know how she died. Once we have, I can answer more of your questions.'

'Make sure you do or I'll be making a formal complaint!' Grant stood, knocked his chair over and stormed out of the office and exited the station.

Sandall looked at Wright. 'But we have the results. Mac has emailed his report.'

'Do you think it would be a good idea to tell him in the mood he is in?'

'No, ma'am, of course not.'

'And,' Wright said, ' there's not a chance in hell he was at a work meeting. Whatever he was doing, it had nothing to do with work.'

In another interview room, Watson sat opposite Marcus Devonport and Steph Parkinson, who were accompanied by their fathers. A female PC was standing by the door.

He cleared his throat before speaking. 'Mr Devonport, Mr Parkinson, Marcus, Steph, thank you for coming in. Now Alison's body has been found, we have many questions and hope you two will answer some of them.'

All four of them nodded.

'Okay. Let's go over what we have.' Watson opened the file in front of him. 'Alison left her house at 8.30 a.m. on Monday for a run. She was reported missing two hours later. Early this morning, her body was found on the railway embankment. We need to find out what happened to her after she went out. So, any information you have, however irrelevant you think it may be, is greatly appreciated.'

He noticed Marcus and Steph exchanging a glance. They knew something.

'Marcus, where were you on Monday morning, prior to turning up at Alison's house?'

Marcus took a deep breath. 'I was at home. I had arranged to meet Alison at eleven o'clock before going into town.'

'And when you arrived, what happened?' He took notes.

'Alison's mum was at the door saying that Alison had not got back, and she was worried. I got into my car and went out to look for her.'

'And you never saw her along the route?'

'No, and I looked all along her route.'

'What car do you drive?' Watson asked.

'Erm a Toyota Aygo, why?'

'Colour?'

'Silver. It was parked outside the house when you first came that morning.'

'Thanks. That helps. If someone remembers seeing a silver Toyota Aygo, we know it was you.' Watson smiled.

'And Steph, did you have any contact with Alison Monday morning? You were at school, I presume?'

'No, I hadn't talked to her since the evening before, when we were all in town. Marcus rang me during maths to tell me Alison was missing.'

'And how was she the evening before?'

Marcus answered. 'She was fine, her normal self. Enjoying the night.'

'Until those boys tried to chat her up,' Steph added.

Watson opened his mouth to follow that up when he heard a commotion outside. He nodded to the PC to check it out before turning back to Steph. 'Tried to chat her up?'

'Yes, typical drunks who think every girl is free game.'

Before Watson could continue, the PC came back in and informed him Wright and Sandall had taken David Grant into another interview room. He nodded.

'Sorry about that,' Watson said. 'What you just heard was Alison's father.'

Marcus and Steph looked at each other with shock on their faces.

'Does he know we're here?' Marcus asked.

'Why do you ask?' Watson queried.

'Because he is a nutter! If he sees us here, he will think we had something to do with Alison's death.' They looked scared.

'Mr Grant has gone into a meeting with my boss. If you want, I will make sure he is still in that meeting or he has left before you go, okay? Why did you say he's a nutter?'

Marcus took a deep breath. 'When he is drunk or when he gets angry, we all keep away from him and that included Alison, her brother, and Mrs Grant. He can be very nasty.'

Mr Devonport spoke up. 'Detective Watson, you see the state of our children. Can we take them home now?'

Watson looked at the parents. 'Just one more question, okay? Marcus, you mentioned Ian Fellows before. Can you tell me more about him?'

'You should keep an eye on him,' Mr Parkinson said. 'It's because of him Steph gave up athletics. Was getting too friendly with her until I warned him off, the bastard.'

'Do you think the same could have happened to Alison?'

Mr Parkinson shrugged. 'I don't know, but it stands to reason, doesn't it?'

Watson crawled through the traffic on his way home. He longed for a quiet evening at home. Family dinner, followed by a curl up on the sofa with Sally, watching some trashy TV programme of her choosing with a bottle of wine. He had given up on watching police series as he would always point out, "That would never happen. They have done that wrong." Sally did the same with the programmes set in schools.

He put on Eric Clapton's *Journeyman* and whacked up the sound to drown out the traffic.

As he pulled into the driveway of his house, he stayed in the car for a few minutes, listening to Eric finishing a superb guitar solo on "No Alibis". A detective's work, he smiled as he got out and walked to the front door.

In the hall, he took off his jacket and exchanged his shoes for slippers. Sally came out of the living room.

'We have a visitor.'

'Who?'

'Simon's manager from the football team.'

'Nick? He's here?' Watson followed Sally.

Nick Thomas had taken over Simon's team when they were in the under-twelves and had been the team's manager for two years now. Under his tutelage, they'd won the second division in his first year. The last season, they had been holding their own in first division. Simon was the midfield dynamo of the team.

Watson walked towards Nick and shook his hand. 'Nick, this is a surprise.'

'I have some exciting news. Ravenswood Rovers have been looking at the under-fourteen league, sending scouts out to matches. This morning I received a letter from them, stating that they were interested in two members of our team. Simon is one of them.'

Simon sat with the biggest smile. Watson looked at him, then Sally. He grinned. 'Who am I to stand in the way of the next Paul Pogba or Frank Lampard?'

Simon jumped up and hugged him, then ran around the room like he had scored the winning goal in the cup final, with Jason and Rachael joining him. Watson signed the permission forms and Nick informed them about the training schedule, match dates, and what was expected of Simon and his parents.

After Nick had left, Watson decided they should celebrate with a meal out. Bang went the lazy evening in front of the TV. He smiled. *I don't mind one bit.*

———

Monteith stormed into the casino, rage in his eyes. He found Lex in the kitchen, pouring a cup of coffee.

'Been anywhere good?' he smirked.

'As you very well know, I've been to my mother-in-law's to see my wife and kids,' Monteith spat.

'I don't know what you mean,' Lex replied, with his back to him, leaving the kitchen and making for the doors to the casino floor.

Monteith grabbed him by the arm and spun him round, spilling the coffee.

Lex narrowed his eyebrows as he looked at Monteith's hand on his arm. 'I suggest you remove that if you don't want it broken.'

Monteith held on. 'You were parked outside the house while I was there. I saw you as I pulled away.'

Lex leaned into Monteith. 'Well if you saw me, there is no point denying it.'

'Leave my family alone,' Monteith bit, jaw tight.

'Oh, threats. I'm scared,' snared Lex. 'I don't know why your wife married a dickhead detective like you; she would have done better marrying me. I would have treated her better.'

Monteith saw red. Enraged, he flew at Lex and punched him in the face. After that, there was no such thing as the Queensberry Rules. Both men went at each other like whirling dervishes. Punches and kicks made their impact as they crashed through the double doors and into the main casino. Staff scattered out of the way as Lex launched Monteith across a table and into the chairs on the other side. Monteith got up and smashed a chair against Lex's torso causing him to double over. Monteith followed up with a kick to the solar plexus. He grabbed Lex and ran him into the front of a fruit machine. Lex slumped to the floor as the machine toppled over. Nobody was going to win a jackpot on that machine tonight.

The security guards broke up the fight and escorted Monteith and Lex to Jimmy Russell's office.

'You said you would leave my wife and family alone.' Monteith was furious. Both he and Lex had cuts and swellings on their faces, bruised knuckles, and torn clothes.

'I gave you my word, and stuck to it.' Russell reclined in his leather-backed chair with his hands, forming a triangle against his chin.

'Then what was this arsehole,' Monteith said, pointing at Lex, 'doing outside of my mother-in-law's house while–'

He never finished his sentence as Lex landed a right-handed punch to his face. Monteith staggered sideways, but then launched himself at Lex. He was caught by Ray and Allan before getting anywhere close.

'STOP!' Jimmy jumped up from his chair and slammed his fist down onto the desk. 'I expect better from my employees. Especially those who I have trusted with more prominent jobs than you both deserve. You two have behaved like bar-room brawlers and you will both pay for the damage downstairs.'

'Get cleaned up, Keith, and then stay in the office and don't come out. Lex, just get out of my sight and go home. I've got important guests coming tonight and I don't want you around when they arrive. Now, piss off.'

Both Monteith and Lex were escorted out of Russell's office. Lex was sent home and Monteith to the bathroom to clean himself up.

A short while later, he had settled into watching the CCTV screens while eating his evening meal of steak and ale pie and chips. His face and body ached, but he was happy he'd given the arsehole a good thrashing, and that he was still standing... Just.

Monteith heard the door to the security office open behind him.

'You certainly gave Lex as good as he gave you,' Ray said, pulling up a chair and relaxing

'Got what he deserved, the wanker.'

Spotting something on a camera, Monteith radioed one of the security officers, 'SO to Bruce, customer at the bar, giving Justine some grief. Check it out, please.'

'As a Londoner, Lex feels he is important. Dropped the A off Alex because he thought it made him sound harder,' Ray explained.

Monteith pointed his fork at Ray. 'He isn't hard. You want hard, go and look at the nutters in the prisons. Some crimes they have been put away for would give you nightmares for the rest of your life.'

'And you gave all that up for sitting in front of a bank of CCTV screens?'

'Wasn't given much of a choice, was I. It was this or end up dead in a ditch somewhere,' Monteith uttered.

'Yes, the boss only makes one-sided deals in his favour. That's why we are working for him.' Ray looked at the floor as he was talking.

Monteith turned to face him. 'He had something on you?'

'He has something on most of us. Yours was gambling, mine...' He didn't appear to be forthcoming.

'And Lex?'

Ray shrugged. 'All I know is that it had something to do with his time in London.'

Monteith made a mental note to check out both men's histories. He was about to pry a bit more but saw from the corner of his eye the tedious customer at the bar again. 'S.O. to Bruce. That prat is giving Justine grief again. Get him out of here.'

He turned back towards Ray, just in time to see the door close behind him.

CHAPTER TEN

Thursday 7 a.m.

ROGER YOUNG WAS UP bright and early. By seven, he was on the road after he had received a call the previous evening asking for help to put a fence up in a nearby village.

His route took him along the back roads, separated from fields with crops by hedges. Little villages with stone-built houses and thatched roofs complemented the countryside Roger so enjoyed. Here, he was safe. No one to bother him. No one to order him around.

Rounding a bend, he slowed down when he saw a car broken down at the roadside. In the driver's seat was a young woman with her phone to her ear. Young signalled and pulled in front of the Alfa Romeo, closer than was needed.

'Can I help you?'

'Oh, thanks ever so much. I'm trying to call my husband and the breakdown service, but I've got no signal. Could you try to make the calls?' She looked at him pleadingly.

'Let's see,' said Young, taking out his phone and pretending to make a call. 'Nope, sorry. Do you want to get in? I could take you to the next village. I'm sure you'll have a better signal there. If not, the newsagent won't mind you calling from the shop.'

The woman hesitated, but then got out of her car and followed Young to his. Opening the door, he invited her to step up into the van. As she put her foot on the sidebar bar to climb in, Young whacked her on the back of the head with a hammer. And again. She collapsed forward against the seat. Young stuffed her into the footwell and covered her with a blanket.

Driving away, Young reflected on the chance meeting. He usually planned these things, but sometimes you had to take advantage of a situation. Lucky for him. Not for the woman in his footwell. The fence would have to wait a little longer.

———

Superintendent Matthews' face looked grim. Clearly, he was not happy, Watson thought. *I hope he will not be difficult.*

'We welcome Superintendent Matthews to this briefing,' Wright started. 'Please, can you update us, DCI Watson?'

He stood and summarised the investigation so far. Turning to French, he said, 'Claire Townsend. Emma, you interviewed the husband yesterday?'

'Yes, gov. Stuart Parker, fiancé, not her husband. He said that their relationship had been on the rocks for some time. Claire had been sleeping with her boss and said she was moving with him to Manchester. Mr Parker assumed she'd done so as he hadn't heard from her since she walked out.'

'Where did she work?'

'At the tyre and exhaust place where her body was found,' Emma answered.

'I want you to go to their HQ and find out where the manager of that place went to in Manchester. Did he take over another garage up there?'

Watson glimpsed at Matthews, who stared into space, a blank expression on his face.

Inwardly sighing, Watson continued, 'Alison Grant. Where are we with her? Paul, you said to me earlier Mac's post-mortem report is available?'

Paul Sandall got up. 'The report found that Alison died from blunt force trauma to the back of the head. She had ligature marks on her wrists and ankles. There were cuts to her face, hands, and knees, believed to have caused by her falling forward on the road surface. She had had intercourse prior to her death; a trace of semen was found. Mac has sent it off to get DNA.'

'It could be from Marcus,' Watson contemplated. 'They were all out on the town the night before she went missing. We need to ask him if they had sex.'

'Also,' Sandall continued, 'A chunk of hair from the back of her head was missing.'

'Hacked off or cut?' Wright asked.

'Definitely cut, and away from the blood-matted part.'

'We have a trophy hunter,' Lorimer grumbled.

'A what?' Sandall looked confused.

'A trophy hunter. Some killers take trophies from their victims, could be a part of clothing like knickers or bra if they are sexual predators. Or body parts like fingers, toes, teeth, and ears.'

'Well done, Karl, for explaining. It also means something else,' Watson's smile faded. 'We could be dealing with a serial killer.'

A silence fell. Everyone looked grim.

PC Barnes put his hand up. 'Sir, a report from one of the squad cars might shed light on where she was taken. A Mr Rose, who was in his front garden tending his roses, would you believe it, told uniform he often saw Alison running past his house on a Monday. If he was in his garden, they would wave to one another. But he didn't see her last Monday.'

'Where along the route is Mr Rose's house?' Watson asked.

'About a half a mile from Alison's house.' Barnes got up and approached the map of the area attached to the wall. 'There. His house is the first of those three.' He pointed to a trio of properties set back from the road, each sporting a large front and ditto back garden.

'That narrows down our search. Let's get CSI out.' Watson looked at Wright, who nodded her agreement. 'Well done, team. This information means we have narrowed down our search area considerably, and that's a start. Has any CSI info come in from the railway embankment?'

'Nothing yet,' Lorimer said.

Roger Young parked his van close to the farmhouse, the passenger side nearest the front door. The snatch had not been planned, but if the gods above gave you a bonus, who was to argue?

He unlocked the front door, after making sure there were no other vehicles on the road. After taping the woman's legs and hands together and applying a strip to her mouth, he lifted her onto his shoulder. Blood had pooled in the footwell and it covered part of her face. He whipped in through the door, slammed the van door, locked it and carried her down to her resting place.

He was late for his job, so the photographs and hair cutting would have to wait.

Within an hour, the CSI team were on the ground, starting their search from the railway line at the back of the estate where the Grants lived. Watson and Sandall parked up on the estate where the cut-through led to the unmanned crossing over the tracks Alison used. The cut-through was less than a hundred metres from the Grants' house. Watson looked around, taking in the surroundings. He knew what the houses were like as they were the same as the one he lived in on the south side of the city. Not as well built as the council houses which were put up when Ravenswood expanded in the seventies but sturdy enough, and with emphasis on providing green spaces and cycle ways for the residents.

'I'd be surprised if she was taken here with all the houses over-looking each other and the road,' Sandall commented.

'If he or she was determined enough, an estate like this would not be a deterrent,' Watson replied. 'Off the road snatches are more common than you think.'

As they got to the end of the cut-through, a goods train trundled past, pulling freight containers. The sound was deafening, and they had to grab hold of the railings as the rush of air almost knocked them sideways.

'Are we looking for anything in particular?' Sandall asked Watson as they walked up the lane.

'From what we know of Mr Rose's report, Alison may have been snatched between here and his house. Mrs Grant told us she listened to music as she ran. But when Alison was found on the embankment, no phone was found. CSI did a good sweep of the area. That means either whoever took her got rid of her phone, which may have been around here, or they still have it.'

Sandall looked at the lane in front of them. CSI were going to have a job finding anything with the amount of things that had been dumped here.

Piles of rubbish, building masonry, and some white goods were among the items stashed in the trees. 'A beautiful area like this and those that don't care just come along and ruin it for everyone.' Sandall shook his head.

'The countryside is a beautiful place until you add one thing,' Watson mused.

Sandall looked at Watson. Simultaneously, they both said, 'Humans.'

They walked along to Mr Rose's house. Nothing stood out among the long grass and thorn ladened hedgerows which could have belonged to Alison.

Mr Rose was standing in his driveway talking to a neighbour. Watson and Sandall approached, flashing the man their ID cards.

'Looks like they have come for you, Frank. It's been nice knowing you,' the neighbour joked.

'Get off, you silly bugger,' Mr Rose chuckled. 'Detectives, what can I do for you?'

'You spoke to our friends in uniform a couple of days ago?'

'Yes, have you found Alison?' Mr Rose asked.

'Unfortunately, we have found her body.' Watson paused. 'We just wanted to go over a couple of things with you, if you don't mind?'

'That's shocking.' Mr Rose shook his head. 'Her parents must be going through hell.'

'You said you saw Alison running most mornings?'

'Yes, when I was in the garden. She would wave at me, either going on her run or coming back. Didn't stop for a chat, though. Concentrating on her running.'

'How busy does this road get around that time in the morning?'

Mr Rose took out a handkerchief and blew his nose before answering. 'Sorry, getting over a cold. Erm just the normal traffic coming out of the village, and farm machinery when the harvest is on.'

'What about vehicles using that dead-end back there?' Sandall asked, pointing over the hedges.

'Fly-tipping alley, you mean,' Mr Rose grumbled. 'Vans and cars with trailers come and go. Mainly during the early hours or late at night when they think no-one will catch them, bloody nuisance they are.'

'Were there any around the day Alison went missing?'

'I can't remember. Oh, hang on. I was talking to our postman, Dave, out here when a lad in a small car stopped to ask a question.'

Watson looked at Sandall.

'What did the lad ask?' Watson quizzed.

'He asked if we had seen a female runner, said he was her friend. We said we hadn't, but would keep an eye out.'

'You don't happen to remember the model or colour of the car, do you?'

'Not the model, but it was silver, if that helps.'

Marcus, Watson thought. He thanked the old man for his help and handed him a card with his contact number on it in case he'd remember anything else.

Walking back, Watson's phone rang.

Seconds later, he turned to Sandall and said, 'CSI have just found a phone with headphones attached to it in the hedge. Let's go.'

They walked towards the hedge where the CSI manager was bagging the phone and earphones and a water bottle in evidence bags.

'They were found in the hedge just over there.' He pointed to his right, where the lane, about thirty yards along from the railway crossing, had been taped off.

Watson looked at the iPhone. Its screen was broken and there were scratches on the back. He pressed the "ON" button, but nothing happened. It was either broken or out of battery. The water bottle was a basic one and still full.

The CSIs resumed their search for evidence, such as dried blood, broken glass, and tyre tread marks to cross-reference them with those found at the railway embankment. Chances were slim they'd find any evidence of a struggle, but they had to be thorough.

Watson took a photo of the evidence bags. 'Time to update the Grants.'

Sitting in the Grants' back garden, Watson observed Joan Grant. She looked gaunt, had sunken, sleepless eyes, and her clothes hung loosely around her. *I cannot image how I'd be*, he thought. *Pure hell.*

He scraped his throat. 'A pity David cannot be here, but a good thing you are, Marcus. The reason we're here is that we've found what we believe to be Alison's phone and water bottle in the hedge by the lane. We need you to confirm it is hers.'

Joan burst into tears at the sight of the picture of the evidence bags he showed her. Marcus came over and hugged her.

'Where did you say you found them?' Joan sobbed.

'Just over the railway line at the back of the estate.'

'Her watch. Have you found her watch?' Joan looked up, wide-eyed.

'No, not yet. What type is it?'

Marcus spoke up, 'I bought her a Fitbit. Keeps track of your heart rate, blood pressure, calculates your steps and a timer to measure distance. It can even track how many hours you sleep.'

Watson looked confused. He hadn't the foggiest idea what Marcus was talking about.

'Does it have GPS?' Sandall asked.

'If you are wondering if we can track the watch, I tried that on my searches and came up with nothing. The range is limited.'

'Talking about your searches,' Watson replied to Marcus. 'Did you speak to anyone while you were out looking for Alison?'

'Oh yes,' Marcus said. 'I asked an old bloke if he had seen Alison. He was talking to a postman by his front gate. He said he saw her most days, but not the day she went missing. I also spoke to a few others, but none of them had seen Alison.'

Watson nodded. 'Based on where we found the phone and water bottle, we believe now she was snatched as soon as she crossed the railway line.'

Joan Grant burst into tears again.

Watson stood up. 'Marcus, walk us out, please?'

As they got to the front door, he asked Marcus. 'I did not want to embarrass you in front of Mrs Grant, but on the Sunday evening when you got back from town, did you and Alison have sex?'

Marcus' face flushed. 'Y- yes, we did.' His eyes suddenly sprang wide open. 'Please, don't tell me she has been raped.'

'Now we have your answer, I can assure you she wasn't.'

CHAPTER ELEVEN

Thursday Noon

WATSON KNOCKED ON THE door of Monteith's house loudly for the second time and stood back. Looking up, he saw the bedroom curtains twitch. He had dropped Sandall off at HQ, instructing him to tell the DSI what they had discovered and to update the whiteboards and HOLMES.

The door opened.

'My God, Keith, you look like hell.'

'You should see the other guy.'

They walked through to the kitchen.

'What the fuck happened to you?' Watson stood leaning against the door frame as Monteith banged the kettle and mugs about.

'One of the so-called bodyguards Russell has, Lex, tried to see how hard I was and regretted it. Can you make the drinks? I need to find some painkillers for this road drill in my head.'

After taking the drinks into the living room, Monteith explained what had happened.

'Sounds like you have made yourself at home with the natives.'

'Monkeys acting like wannabe gorillas.' Monteith snorted his disdain.

'And you come in all alpha male, breaking Lex's nose.'

'Up till now I have behaved myself. Said "yes sir" and "no sir", done what they asked me.'

Watson laughed, 'You've never said "Yes, sir" in your life!'

'There is one big difference between Matthews and Jimmy Russell. One has my balls in a vice and can take away my job, the other has my balls in a vice and can take away my life. And that of my family.'

'Point taken.' Watson raised his mug when he suddenly remembered Monteith had asked him to check out a man. He shouted at Monteith, who had gone back into the kitchen, 'Remember you asked me to check on someone called Tommy Burke?'

Monteith stuck his head around the door. 'Yes, anything?'

'Ten broken fingers – didn't want to name his attackers.'

'What a surprise. NOT.' Monteith came out of the kitchen, carrying a plate of toast. Licking his fingers, he handed Watson an envelope.

'What's in here?'

'That is your next task, detective. CCTV photos of Lex and Ray, the Russells' bodyguards, henchmen, drivers, whatever you call them. Lex is from London; his father was in the force there as a detective. Got done for a protection racket and killed himself in prison. Don't know much about Ray. Local, I think.'

'And this?' Watson held up a CD.

'That is a copy of an incident in the casino the other night. We caught a lad peddling drugs. Allan Russell and Lex dealt with him. You will find out how at the end.'

'I take it, it wasn't a slapped wrist? Did you catch the lad's name?'

'Wayne Marsh, I think. Can't be certain.'

Watson shot a look at Monteith. 'Wayne Marsh?'

'Yes. Why?'

'Because when I was last at Mac's, a lad with that name was brought in. He was found in the park. Possible overdose.'

Monteith balled his fists. 'Bastards,' he shouted. 'Lex force-fed him the ecstasy tablets he was trying to sell. It's all on that disc.'

The black Range Rover Evoke was parked up in one of the visitors' parking spaces outside the council offices. In the back, Jimmy Russell sat expressionlessly, staring straight ahead. He hated days like this, days when he was not in control. When he was could not influence the outcome of meetings. He looked across at the main door, waiting for Ray. Nothing. Checking his watch for the twentieth time, he cursed the council planning committee for being the slowest cumbersome inept run council office. He had considered running for a council position, but he figured politicians and councillors were bigger crooks than him.

Finally, Ray appeared,seat, walking briskly across the car park. Getting into the driver's seat, he lent back and handed Jimmy a note.

Jimmy took one look at it. 'Drive me back to the casino. We have work to do.'

Driving back to the office, Watson spotted Joseph Clayton standing at a bus stop. Clayton was looking all of his seventy-plus years: tired and haggard. *Life was not good to you in recent times. And chasing after your two loony sons does not help.*

He turned his car around and pulled up next to Joseph. He wound down the side window. 'Need a lift?'

'Oh, Mr Watson. Yes, thanks for the offer, I'm off back home.' Joseph picked up his shopping and walking cane and got in the front passenger seat. 'You're a saviour, Mr Watson. The buses can be a pain, especially when they are busy. The young people don't have respect for the elderly. Not bothering to get up when there are no seats.'

Watson signalled to move back into the traffic. 'Where're your boys, Davy and Billy? Don't they help you out, give you a lift into town?'

Joseph grunted. 'They're off doing their things. Anyway, on my own I can have a quick pint and a bet on the horses.'

Watson laughed. 'Nothing like keeping your hand in with both of them.'

'How's your family?' Joseph enquired.

'Very well, thank you. Jason turned twelve the other day.'

'Really! How time flies.' Joseph shook his head.

After fifteen minutes, they arrived at the Thelwell Estate where Joseph lived. Joseph turned to him. 'I hear you're having another go at the Russells?'

'Don't know what you have heard but...'

'Oh, come now, Mr Watson. The grapevine is long at the moment. Nothing gets past us nowadays.'

He glanced at Clayton. 'Sorry, Joseph, cannot comment.'

'Is that why Mr Monteith has not been around for a while?'

Watson glanced at him. 'No comment.'

'Suit yourself,' Joseph grinned widely.

Watson parked outside his house.

'Can you help me in with my shopping? I feel a little out of breath.'

Watson smiled; he had a soft spot for the old man. 'Open the door, I'll grab your bags.' He noticed the curtains were twitching in the neighbouring houses as he made his way into the property.

'I would just love to give them something to really get the gossipers going. Standing fully naked in front of my bedroom window would do it.'

'And you would end up with time in our cells and a trip to court. Now, where do you want this shopping?'

'It's my house. I can walk around naked if I want. On the kitchen side and put the kettle on while you are at it.'

Watson walked back into the front room. 'The kettle's on and I need to get going.'

Joseph settled in his chair by the fireplace. 'Hang on a minute, Mr Watson.'

Watson turned to Joseph with a puzzled expression.

He continued. 'Can you go into my bureau behind my chair? Second drawer down, there is an envelope marked confidential.'

Watson did as instructed and passed it to Joseph. 'No, you take it, Mr Watson. It's for you and your team.'

'What's in it?' Watson asked, curious now.

Joseph took a big breath and looked straight at Watson. 'If you are looking to take down the Russells, what's in there will hopefully help you. I've known the Russells since they arrived here in the 70s. Their father was not a man to cross. And his sons, as you know, carried on the tradition. In that envelope are photocopies of a book

I had stashed away. My insurance, so to speak. What you have there are details of the Russells' activities I have collected over the years. Loose lips in the pub bragging, petty feuds. Some you may know about but could not pin on them. Some... Well, have a read.'

Watson tapped the envelope. 'How do you know about all of this? Providing what you have given me is true and not made up.'

Joseph feigned a hurtful look. 'Mr Watson! Just hurt me in your accusations. Let's just say I like to keep my friends close and my enemies closer.'

<hr />

When Watson arrived at the office, Wright asked him to join her and French and Lorimer in her office. Watson took both Clayton's and Monteith's envelop and walked into his boss' office.

'Emma and Karl will not be here for the next couple of days,' Wright announced, even before he had sat down.

'That's going to leave us a bit thin on the ground, ma'am.'

'I know, but it can't be helped. The National Tyre Company sent us through the employee list for their garage in Copeland. The manager, Nigel Prior, transferred to a garage in Salford, in Greater Manchester, just after it closed. Matthews has signed off on them going up there to interview Prior. Contact has been made with the county force up there, so they know our presence.'

'That only leaves me, Sandall, and PC Barnes. Assuming we still have him?'

'Yes, we do. Emma, Karl, you two get off and pack. We booked two rooms at a local Premier Inn; they've been made aware you may arrive late.'

'Oh boss, you spoilsport.' Lorimer pretended to be disappointed. French punched him in the arm.

'It's bad enough I have to share a car with you. You think I was going to share a room as well?' French smiled and followed him out the door.

Watson looked at Wright with curiosity.

'Have you not noticed the spark between the two of them?'

'And you're letting them go to Manchester together? They will either come back married or dead.'

'As long as the one still living brings back Nigel Prior,' Wright grinned. She got out of her chair behind the desk and moved to sit in the one next to Watson. Watson divulged his theory that Alison had disturbed someone fly-tipping and was killed to shut her up.

'Wrong place, wrong time. That's a huge leap.' Wright didn't look convinced.

'It's a long shot, I know. The other is that whoever murdered her knew her route, when she would be running, that she'd be alone and that hardly anybody would be around. Now that's something I don't want to be correct on.'

Wright nodded.

'Paul Sandall looks like he is settling in well. He updated me on what you found and the interview with Mr Rose and Mrs Grant.'

'Yes, he's going places, that one,' Watson acknowledged. 'But ma'am, I have something else to discuss. I met Joseph Clay on my way in and he gave me an envelope with, as he indicated, facts about the Russells' activities. Said the original is stashed away somewhere for insurance. It seems the Claytons and the Russells go way back. I have not looked at it yet.'

'Do you think it might provide interesting information?' Wright said sceptically.

'I have known Joseph for as long as I have been here and, although his family aren't always on the right side of the law, when Joseph says something like that, he means it. Both the Russell and Clayton families have been in Ravenswood since the 1970s. Maybe it contains evidence of crimes Jimmy and Allan's father has committed and it may tie up some unsolved cold cases. Although, as he died in the early 2000s, a prosecution would not happen. But if Jimmy and Allan themselves were involved, well, that's a different matter.' He handed Wright the envelope.

'Then Keith. I went to check on him earlier. He was looking worse for wear. Settling in with the natives. Got in a fight yesterday with one of Russells' goons. The bloke deserved it.'

'He hasn't been found out?' Wright looked worried.

'No, or I would have pulled him out straightaway.' Watson opened the envelope Monteith had given him and handed two photos to Wright. 'These two are the Russells' go-to guys, drivers, bodyguards, you name it. The ones who dumped Keith after his abduction. Their names are Lex and Ray. Keith put what he knows about them on the backs of the photos. He's made a good connection with Ray, who told him that the Russells have something against each of them tucked away on file. Lex is the hard man and the one Keith had a fight with.'

Wright glanced over to Barnes' desk. She knocked on the partition window and gestured for him to come over.

'Can you run a facial recognition on these two? Check their backgrounds and see if they have any convictions.'

'Yes, ma'am.'

Watson continued. 'This disc shows what Lex is capable of.' Wright took the disc and put it into her computer. They watched the CCTV pictures Monteith had pieced together.

'This Lex guy is one evil bastard,' Wright exclaimed. 'Who's the suit he spoke to before leaving the casino?'

'Keith said it was Allan Russell.'

'So, we can get both Allan Russell and Lex for... What happened to the man?'

'Murder. The lad they force-fed the tablets was found dead in the park. Mac has his body. The post-mortem suggests a drugs overdose. We now know it wasn't an accidental one.'

'I can go with that, but we don't want to arrest them with Keith still being there though, so we'll have to hang till a while longer. Besides, we'd have to disclose the CCTV images during their interview and they'd know Keith had shared it. It puts his life and his family's in danger. I'll update Matthews. After the way he was this morning, this should get off our backs.'

Watson nodded. 'Hopefully, the Clayton intel will blow the Russells case wide open and we can get Keith out of there. Can't happen soon enough, if you ask me.'

A knock on the door interrupted them. Sandall stuck his head in. 'Sorry to bother you. Report has come in; we have another missing woman. About a mile from where Alison Grant was taken.'

Jimmy Russell sat behind his large oak desk, swirling the finest scotch in his crystal glass. He was surrounded by every bit of refinery money could buy, but all he could think about was the fight between

Lex and Monteith. Fighting, unless sanctioned by him, was a sackable offence. He had thrown out employees for less and taught them the error of their ways on leaving. Was he getting soft? *Not a cat in hell's chance.* Not with what he had planned. He got up and stood in front of Lex and Monteith.

'You two are disappointments. If it was anyone else who behaved like you did, they'd be lying in hospital beds with feeding tubes down their throats after I'd finished with them. You two are on a final warning; any more and you won't even be needing a bleeding hospital. Got it?'

'Yes, boss,' they both responded.

'Piss off to either end of the casino and keep out of each other's way until tonight. I have a job for you to do later. Thanks to another numbskull not doing his properly, a visit is needed.'

Jimmy handed Ray a piece of paper. 'You know what to do?'

Ray nodded and left.

CHAPTER TWELVE

Thursday Afternoon

A FEELING OF DÉJÀ VU overcame Watson as he and Sandall surveyed the area. A back road out of a village, not much traffic, looking for a missing woman. This time they had more to go on: a car.

They had been let through the police cordon, set up at the end of the road leading out of the village of Little Beck. Parking up, they could see an Alfa Romeo covered with a forensic tent. A smaller one was erected close by. They signed the register of attendance and made their way across to the squad cars.

'Afternoon, sir, I'm PC Andrew Murray.'

'What have we got?' Watson asked, looking around.

'We have Samantha's husband, Craig Field, in the back of the squad car. The car is his wife's. Her office called him about noon, as she hadn't shown up for work. After Mr Field tried unsuccessfully to reach her, he left work and went home. When she wasn't there, he started following the route she would have taken and found her car abandoned here. He has given us a description of Samantha and a photo. We have informed the station so other uniforms can look out for her.'

Watson and Sandall thanked the officer and approached the squad car.

'You can take this, Paul,' Watson encouraged the newbie detective.

Sandall slid in next to the husband. 'Mr Field? My name is DC Sandall, and this is DCI Watson.'

Craig Field nodded and whispered, 'Hello.' There were tear stains on his cheeks.

'Mr Field, your wife's description has been circulated across the media and we are looking out for her,' Sandall said.

The man nodded.

'Is there anything else you can tell us which may help us locate your wife? Anywhere she might have gone. A friend she might have visited?'

Craig shook his head. 'No, she was supposed to be in the office.'

'I'm sorry to ask this. How were things between you two?'

Field looked straight at Sandall. 'Our marriage was fine, just celebrated our second anniversary. Spent last weekend away, at a hotel,' he replied, getting out of the car.

The Crime Scene Manager came over and pulled Watson aside. 'We've taken hair, fabric, and skin cell fragment samples and fingerprints from outside the car, to compare against Mr Field's. We need to look inside, but it's all locked up. Can you witness us if we have to break the window?'

'One moment.' He strode over to Field. 'Do you have the spare key to your wife's car with you?'

'Actually I do,' the man replied. 'We have one for each other in case we lose them.' He handed it over, then exclaimed, 'Shit.'

'What is it?'

'I had completely forgotten. We had a motion activated dash-cam fitted to Sam's car three months ago when the insurance needed renewing. Got a discount for having one.'

A Crime Scene Investigator pressed the key fob and opened the car. Noticing a round smear on the window but no camera, she checked the footwell with her gloved hand. Retrieving the camera, she said, 'We may have a recording of what happened to Samantha.'

———

'And Watson got this from Joseph Clayton?' Chief Superintendent Matthews asked. He frowned and looked again at the two sheets of paper on his desk. Specifically, two lines halfway down the second sheet.

'Yes, that's right,' Wright replied. 'Clayton said it was his security; these are copies of the original which he has stashed somewhere.'

'Has Watson seen this?' Matthews asked in disbelief.

'No. He would have said something if he had, especially after what we have just read. Joseph Clayton is a reliable source, sir. He's helped the agency in the past.'

'The information helps the Claytons. I'm not that wet behind the ears, DSI Wright. Is DS Monteith still under cover?'

'Yes. DCI Watson saw him this morning. He was a bit worse for wear after an altercation last night.'

'Is he alright?'

'Yes, from what Watson told me. DS Monteith also gave us information about two of Russell's bodyguards, which we are looking into right now. Should be ready for tomorrow morning's briefing.'

'Where is Watson now?'

'Dealing with a woman gone missing, out at Little Beck. He should be back soon,' Wright said, looking at her watch.

'When he comes in, bring him up here. This stays between the three of us until we can confirm or counter any of it. If this gets out, the press will have a field day.'

'Of course. Can I have some more manpower to do the checks on the other pieces of info? PC Barnes is already looking into Allan Russell's cronies, and with Lorimer and French in Manchester, we are a bit stretched.' Wright put on her best stressed and overworked look.

'I will see what I can do.'

Watson and Sandall left Little Beck just after 4.30 p.m. They had seen uniform drive off, escorting Craig Field home. The CSI were packing up and the dash-cam footage was wending its way across town to be viewed. Samantha Field's car was being loaded onto a lorry to be brought to the force's own garage for a forensic examination.

'I was impressed at the Grants' house, Paul,' Watson remarked. 'When you were talking to Marcus about that thing you called a Fitbit. Went straight over my head.'

'Fitbits are fitness trackers you wear on your wrist. They can track your heart rate, help with exercise workouts, and monitor how many calories you burn, how many steps you take. Very useful.'

Watson looked confused. 'The only thing I wear on my wrist is this watch. My exercise is chasing criminals or running the line for my son Simon's football team. I have not seen the inside of a gym since police training. I know my heart is working because I have not dropped dead yet. I seem to be an analogue man trapped in a digital world with all this new tech stuff that's coming out. Downloading music, instead of holding and playing CDs or vinyl.' Watson grabbed hold of the CD he was playing in the car and handed it to Sandall.

Who are Pink Floyd? You must be old listening to this,' Sandall grinned.

'Cheeky! Touché.' Watson smiled as he turned the car into the fly tip alley.

'Why are we here again? I thought CSI had gone over this?' It was Sandall's turn to be confused.

Watson parked up, 'Lesson one at being a good detective. Always go over the scene one last time if things don't feel right. And this doesn't feel right.'

Both men got out of the car.

'What are we looking for?'

'You will know when you see it,' responded Watson.

For the next fifteen minutes, they searched everything, including the things that had been fly-tipped. Sandall stopped and crouched down by a pile of rubble just inside a field.

'Sir! Over here,' Sandall beckoned.

Watson jogged across. 'What have you got?'

Sandall crouched and pulled away some fencing that had been tossed on the ground. 'When we were at the Grants', I noticed they'd had part of their fencing replaced, and it looked quite recent. I remember the name on their panels.'

Watson looked at him. 'Carry on.'

'What if the person who fixed the fence was the one who took Alison? He came along here because he had watched her previously, knew her route. What if they dumped the old broken panels here and then waited for her?' Sandall's face was flushed with excitement.

'It's a good theory, Paul. Can you see a name on the panels?'

Sandall showed him. 'Yes. It's the same one on the Grants' panels. Roger Young.'

Thursday Evening

Roger Young unlocked the door to his prize. He had been visualising her throughout his working day. Her smell. The pictures he would take for his collection. Her hair, a piece of which would end up in a little plastic box on the shelf.

The boss at the site he had been working had been a pain in the arse, nitpicking his work. The fence posts were the wrong type and put in the wrong place, bla bla bla. He wanted to stick a post where the sun didn't shine by the end of the day.

She was still where he had laid her on the mattress. She had moved slightly, possibly through drifting in and out of consciousness.

He took his camera and started taking photographs. He didn't know her name; this had been an instinctive one. The ones before had been planned, so he'd known them. He finished snapping photos and picked up the large scissors. Finding a chunk of hair which had not been polluted with blood, he removed it with precision. He held it in his hands and sniffed, taking a deep breath to inhale her unique fragrance.

After cutting off a few more strands, he put a few strands aside and the rest in a small plastic box. The date and where he'd picked her up were written on the front. Satisfied, he placed the box on the shelving alongside the others. Opening a drawer, he put the remaining strands in there, along with the rest he had collected. He would start on the next phase tonight.

Watson and Wright were waiting for Matthews outside his office. Much to his PA's annoyance, that was clear.

Matthews opened his door and beckoned them in, saying goodnight to Beryl at the same time. Watson and Wright followed Matthews into his office.

'Did DSI Wright tell you why I wanted to see you?'

'Only that it had something to do with what Joseph Clayton had given to me,' Watson responded, not sure what Matthews was hinting at.

'What exactly were Joseph Clayton's words when he handed you the envelope?' Matthews asked.

'He said that if we were looking to take down the Russells, what's in there would help us. Photocopies of a book he has stashed away as insurance.' Watson looked at both Wright and Matthews. 'What *was* in it?'

'You have not looked at it prior to this evening?'

'No, I handed it over to DSI Wright as soon as I came back. Why? What's in it?' Watson felt nervous. He flicked his eyes between his two bosses.

Matthews opened a file on his desk and removed two sheets of paper. He leaned over, handing them to Watson. 'The second sheet halfway down. I marked it.'

Watson glanced at the marked passage. *This can't be true!* He was dumbstruck. 'You're kidding, right? It's... it's impossible. A joke!'

'This is obviously new to you. Do you think DS Monteith knows?'

Watson shook his head vehemently. 'No. No, sir. He would have told me. This changes everything. I don't like it. He could be in danger.'

'You're right,' Matthews acknowledged. 'Now that the level of risk has gone up, we need to strike earlier than planned.'

'May I suggest something?' Wright interrupted. 'Why don't Terry and I visit Joseph Clayton and get this info confirmed. Once we know more, we can draw up a plan of action.'

Matthews was silent. He fiddled with his pen, then said, 'I agree. As soon as possible.'

Watson and Wright left Matthews' office and walked down to their floor. As they entered, Sandall signalled them.

'That was CSI. They have viewed that dashcam footage and it's dynamite.'

An hour later, the full force of the Ravenswood police service was outside Roger Young's farm. Wright, Watson, and Sandall were accompanied by Armed Response Unit officers. An ambulance was parked nearby. DSI Wright was talking to the head of the ARU to establish the best way to breach the farmhouse. Young's van was parked close to the house and could be used as cover.

Wright returned from her chat with the ARU coordinator.

'We are going in. Checks have been completed to the barn over there, which was clear, and the van. They've found blood underneath the passenger side door. Not too much, so hopefully, Samantha Field is still alive. Assuming it's her he took. Get ready.'

As quickly and as quietly as the uniformed and armed police could go, they surrounded the front of the farmhouse. Wright, Watson, and Sandall stood back until the front door was forced open with a battering ram.

An officer swung the enforcer at the door's locks. The door shattered with a loud crack as the wood splintered.

'Armed police! Armed police! Stay where you are!'

Helmeted and vested men and women stormed through the gap where the front door had been seconds before, to secure the area. Roger Young was sitting at the kitchen table. They brought him to the floor and cuffed him. Officers split up to search the house, bolting through the doors of each room. Footsteps bounded above them, followed by shouts of 'Clear!'

Wright, Watson, and Sandall entered the kitchen. Young had been picked up and put back on the chair. Two officers stood behind him.

'Where is Samantha Field, Mr Young?' Wright asked.

'Who?' Young snarled back, but Watson spotted a quick flick of his eyes towards the door under the staircase.

'Boss, the door,' he said, pointing to it. 'Where's the key?'

Sandall grabbed a bunch of keys off the table and lobbed them to Watson. Three tries later, they were in. Watson leading the charge down the stairs and turned the light on. He stopped dead in his tracks. Wright bumped into him.

'What...' She fell silent.

The walls were covered with photographs of bound and gagged terrified women.

'Watson!' Wright pointed to a door inside the basement. He turned around.

Fiddling with the keys, he found the right one, slotted it into the lock and shoved the door wide.

'GET PARAMEDICS DOWN HERE NOW!' he bellowed.

In the corner was Samantha Field, tied and bound, lying on a soiled mattress. Instinctively, Watson moved forward but Wright held him back.

'This is a crime scene, Terry. Don't touch anything.'

The paramedics pushed their way into the room and rushed towards Samantha.

'She's alive, but only just,' one of them called out. The other – gloved and ready to hand the bindings to the police to bag as evidence – started removing the ties around her wrists and feet, and the tape across her mouth. She didn't show any response.

'We need to move her fast.'

Watson balled his fists and turned to exit the basement. Wright grabbed his arm. 'Calm down Terry, we've got him, and we have saved her. There is no need to run around. Let's leave the medics and read Young his rights.'

'He does not deserve any rights,' Watson said through gritted teeth.

'Stay professional. We don't want to give the CPS a reason to question our behaviour or, worse, the evidence.'

Back in the kitchen, Watson, feeling sick and disgusted, read Young his rights.

'Get him out of here!' he said when he finished.

The paramedics left soon after with Samantha, the ambulance wailing, blue lights spinning. A CSI team arrived and taped off and photograph Young's van and the land surrounding the property.

'How many do you think he's taken?' Sandall asked.as they inspected the photographs.

'There were at least ten women pictured on these walls,' Wright sighed.

'Including Alison Grant!' Watson exclaimed, pointing at her photograph. All three of them fell silent. *What was there to say? It was all just sickening. The photos, the shelves of boxed hair, the soiled stinking mattress...* The CSI team would need all night to go through it all.

In the car on the drive back to the headquarters, Wright ordered, 'I want you two to go home when we get back. Young is not going anywhere, and we have twenty-four hours to charge him. Tomorrow morning, I want you to be on your game in that interview room.'

Watson was glad to go home. He felt a massive headache coming on. The thought of working into the early hours of the night hadn't been helping. His mind was a mess and the words he'd read on that piece of paper reverberated in his head.

Keith Monteith is Jimmy and Allan Russell's half-brother

At home, in his den, Watson stared into a blank. Joseph had said the info was his insurance. Friends close, enemies closer. The Russells were nobody's friends. First the father, now the sons. Not to be messed with.

He glanced up to see Sally leaning against the doorframe. 'You look so serious. What are you pondering about?'

'Info Joseph Clayton gave me earlier. About the Russells.'

'Everything at the moment seems to have something to do with that family,' Sally exclaimed. 'Keith and Katie would still be together if it wasn't for them. She's in bits over at her mum's. And the kids cannot understand why daddy is not with them.'

He got up from his desk and put his arms around Sally. 'It's complicated.'

'Try telling that to Katie and the kids.'

'Keith did. It was Katie's choice to move out.'

'So, it was Katie's fault, was it?'

'No, I didn't say that. Keith was put in a no-win situation.'

'Well, he wouldn't have been in that situation if it wasn't for his gambling.'

'You'll not get an argument from me.' He pulled Sally close and gave her a hug. 'Listen, why we are getting heated up over this? I can think of something better to do.' He kissed her passionately.

'Oh, you can, can you?'

His lips moved from her mouth to her neck.

Sally moaned. 'You better follow me then.' Taking his hand, they walked towards the stairs.

CHAPTER THIRTEEN

Friday 2 a.m.

'DON, DON, SOMEONE'S IN the house. Don, wake up!'

Angela Spedding was in bed, shaking with fear. Her husband was a deep sleeper. She turned her bedside light on.

'What the bloody hell are you doing?' Don rolled away but got caught in the duvet.

'Don, there is someone in the house. I heard noises downstairs.' She shook him again making sure he stayed awake.

'Stop it,' Don said. He turned back, leaning on both elbows, squinting against the light, his hairy chest visible above the duvet.

'Haven't you heard me? There is someone in the house!' Angela's voice was shrill.

'It's your imagination; you should stop reading those Tony Forder thrillers before coming to bed. It's doing your head in,' Don grumbled.

They froze. Something was crashing downstairs.

'I told you,' Angela whispered.

'Shut up, woman.' Don threw back the duvet and reached behind the wardrobe for his baseball bat. 'Stay there,' he said, creeping around the bed to the door. Opening it just a crack, he took a peek out onto the landing. Not seeing anything, he opened the door wider and checked further round to the stairs. At the bottom, he spotted glass fragments and flowers scattered over a pool of water.

Tip-toeing down the stairs, Don reached the bottom. Manoeuvering around the broken glass, he carefully opened the front room and switched on the light. It had been ransacked.

He raised his bat and stepped forward. The door slammed shut behind him and he felt a whack on his head with something heavy. Don dropped the bat and grabbed at his head, stumbled, and fell to the ground. The intruder hit him again, sending him into darkness.

Angela had followed Don down the stairs and started screaming. The intruder turned and looked at her. His accomplice came out of the kitchen. Both were wearing balaclavas and were dressed in black. Angela shrieked again and ran back upstairs. The intruders both bolted up the stairs after her, pushing the bedroom door open before she could lock it. She ran to the window and opened the curtains, shouting for help. One of the intruders picked her up and threw her on the bed.

'What the fuck are you doing?' Monteith shouted through his balaclava at Lex.

'Just making sure the message is received,' Lex said, looking at Angela Spedding as he approached the bed.

'I'm out of here; we've done what we came for,' Monteith said furiously, moving for the door.

'Getting scared, are we?' Lex laughed.

'Piss off,' Monteith raged as he ran down the stairs. He didn't want to be here in the first place, but they had given him no choice. Reaching the bottom stairs, he checked on Don Spedding. The man was out cold. The pictures they had left, still on the table. He heard the man's wife's shrill as he ran out of the back door and onto the narrow passageway backing the houses.

'He's fucking off his head!' Monteith exclaimed, jumping into the back of the Range Rover.

'Where's Lex?' Ray asked from the driver's seat.

'According to him, making sure the message is received by doing whatever he is doing to Spedding's wife.' Monteith was fuming. He knew there was a chance he could get dragged into the Russells' dealings, but issuing beatings was not on that list.

'He's becoming a liability,' Ray said, staring out of the windscreen. 'There have been a few times he has gone over the top when we were out on business.'

Monteith was just about to press Ray for more info when Lex came lumbering out of the shadows and jumped into the front of the car. Ray pulled out of their hiding place.

'That was fun,' Lex grinned while taking off his balaclava.

'Tell me she is still alive?' Ray spat the question out.

'Course she is.' Looking back at Monteith, 'What did this wimp tell you? I was killing her?' Lex laughed. 'She passed out after I slapped her a couple of times.'

'And Don?'

'He'll wake up with a headache. Now let's get back and have a drink.'

Monteith sat in the back seat.

I've had enough.

Friday 7.30 a.m.

The smell of bacon and sausage baps made Watson's mouth water as he entered the office. He was closely followed by Sandall and Barnes. They spotted DSI Wright and Chief Superintendent Matthews eating.

'Don't stand on ceremony, lads,' Matthews said. 'There's plenty to go round. We have a big day in front of us and I thought a hearty breakfast would be in order.' it momentarily rendered Watson speechless.

'Get over here or we will eat the lot,' Wright advised.

That was enough to get him moving.

'Lorimer and French will not like having been left out of this,' Sandall spoke through a mouthful of bacon and bread.

'Lorimer and French are not here. Anyway, Frenchie is a vegetarian,' Watson corrected him.

'Keep eating, but let's get down to business,' Matthews said. 'I have been told that Roger Young had a visit from an on-call solicitor last night; she will come back in an hour. Do we have all the facts in order for the interview?'

Wright picked up two files and handed them to Watson.

'In there, you will find the details of what CSI found on Samantha Field's car, fingerprints, etc. As well as what we've found out of her abduction from the dash cam footage. That is just for starters. Prelim report from Young's van found Samantha's blood on the passenger side footwell and on a hammer and blanket found within the vehicle. So, we've got enough evidence to charge him with abduction, GBH, and false imprisonment to start with.'

'How is Samantha?'

'Had a call at seven this morning from PC Walker, who has been guarding her overnight. Samantha is on life support after an operation to remove a blood clot in her brain. Skull fractured in three places. Doctors say it is still too early to say if she will survive because of the time she spent unconscious and without medical attention.'

'Anything from CSI regarding Alison Grant? She must have been there because her photograph was on his wall, alongside the others.'

'Not yet. They concentrated on Samantha Field first. I will get back to them this morning. Young is not going anywhere, so can we make sure we have clear-cut evidence he took Alison. The CPS will not press charges just because he has a picture of her on his wall. The same goes for the other women.'

She turned to Barnes. 'When you have finished collecting the information on Lex and Ray, can you look at reports of missing women, and see which ones match the photographs on Young's wall? We need to make a start on that this morning.'

'Yes, boss. I have a couple of things to check over on Lex and Ray first. It has been very interesting doing the background checks on them,' Barnes said.

'And we need those things on Joseph Clayton's list to be checked out as well,' Watson reminded them.

Wright checked the time. It was 8.15 a.m. 'Okay, Terry, you interview Young. Take Paul with you. I think you're in room three. Barnes, come with me for an update on Lex and Ray.'

Matthews followed Watson and Sandall out of the main office. 'I hear good things about you, Detective Constable Sandall, keep it up.' He turned and started the stairs to the fourth floor.

Sandall stood gobsmacked.

'Close your mouth, I can see that last sausage bap you had.' Watson chuckled. 'See, news travels fast if you keep your head down and do your job. On the other hand, if you screw up, it seems to get around even quicker, so be watchful.'

The lounge curtains were still closed at 8 a.m. as the postman pushed the envelopes through the letterbox. Nothing stirred from within the house. Monteith did not move from his seat. The nightly scene kept replaying through his head.

Things are out of hand. I'm out of my depth.

Monteith stared at the sunshine filtering through the crack between the curtains. He picked up his phone. Hesitated. Then he rapidly typed.

Need to see you urgently. Things got out of hand last night. Need to get pulled out NOW.

Roger Young had been brought up from the cells and had put into interview room three. His solicitor was waiting for him. Watson and Sandall gave them ten minutes before starting the interview process. Watson took one last look at his phone before going in and spotted Monteith's text.

'Just a moment Paul, I need to make a call. Let them sweat a couple more minutes.' Watson nipped down the corridor and dialled Monteith.

''Bout time you called,' Monteith fired.

'Sorry, didn't see it and I'm just about to go into an interview. Tell me what's wrong.'

'I helped in a visit last night on behalf of the Russells.'

'WHAT?' Watson was not sure he'd heard that properly.

'I was told I had to accompany Lex and Ray to someone who had pissed off the Russells,' Monteith said slowly, in a monotone voice.

Watson felt shocked. noticed Sandall and Wright looking at him, waiting.

'Can you make it in here without the Russells knowing? I need to go into this interview but will see you after here then. Okay?'

'I will try. I'm scared, Terry, I want out.'

'I got you, mate. We'll sort it.' Watson ended the call and turned to Wright.

'Keith. He's coming in. Something happened last night.'

Wright looked at him. 'Okay, Terry, interview Young. I'll talk to Keith when he gets in.'

'Thank you, ma'am,' Watson said, as he walked into the interview room, followed by Sandall.

Both pulled their chairs out opposite Young and his solicitor. Sandall informed them that the interview was being recorded on audio and video. After introducing themselves, Watson reminded Young that he was still under caution.

'Mr Young, can you tell me about your movements yesterday? Say from 7 a.m. to 5 p.m?'

'I was at work.'

'And where was that and what do you do for work?'

'I am a self-employed fencer and was working over at a new build over at Big Beck.'

'You were there all day?'

'Yes.'

'If we spoke to the site foreman there, they'd vouch for you?'

'Yes.'

'Mr Young, on your way to work, do you remember seeing an Alfa Romeo broken down on the road between Little Beck and Big Beck?'

Young frowned. 'Yes. The driver was on the phone, so I drove past.'

'You went past? Did you not stop?'

'No.'

'For the record, I am showing Mr Young and his solicitor evidence record RY1 and RY2.' Watson opened his file and removed two evidence bags containing photographs, which he placed on the table in front of Roger Young. His solicitor leaned forward to inspect them. Watson put his hand up and continued.

'These photographs have been taken from the broken-down Alfa Romeo's dash cam recording. The Alfa Romeo that you just told me you drove past, not stopping to assist the driver who'd broken down. Is that your work van in both pictures?' Watson looked Young straight in the eyes.

'No comment,' Young replied, glancing at his solicitor.

'Is that your van parked up in front of the Alfa?'

'No comment.'

Watson brought out of the file two more pictures. 'Mr Young, is that you getting out of your van and coming towards the driver's side door of the Alfa Romeo?'

The solicitor looked at the pictures. 'Can I have some time with my client, please?'

Watson nodded.

Sandall said, 'Interview suspended,' and stopped the recording.

Watson got up to leave. He turned, 'Just to let you know we have enough to charge Mr Young for the abduction of the driver of the Alfa Romeo. It's the other nine women who he has pictures of that we want information on.' With that, he and Sandall left the room, leaving a PC standing guard.

They met up with Wright in the corridor. 'Interesting but not surprising that he switched to "no comment" after you'd shown him the photos,' she pointed out.

'I expected nothing less. He's not going anywhere, and he knows it. He just wants to drag his heels for as long as he can,' Watson said confidently. 'I suggest we see if CSI has come through with anything else that we can get him on before we continue the interview.'

The three of them made their way back upstairs to the main office. Barnes, who was holding fort, turned from his computer as they entered the incident room.

'Just heard from Lorimer and French about ten minutes ago. They went to talk to Nigel Prior, and he caved in and admitted to killing Claire Townsend. They have arrested him and are arranging for transport to bring him back here for an interview.'

'Well, that's at least some good news today,' Wright smiled weakly.

'Have CSI come back with anything else on the other women?' Sandall asked Barnes, as he tucked into a cold bacon bap.

'Funny you should say that.' Barnes picked up a report from his desk. 'Fingerprints on Alison Grant's water bottle and phone match Young's; blood and hair found on a mattress inside Young's van match Alison's DNA. They are looking at the mattress from the house, but there are a lot of bodily fluids, skin cell fragments and hair samples, so it may take a while to distinguish one profile from another.'

'That's two he's going down for.' Watson punched the air.

'We have to get it past the CPS first.' Wright reminded everyone. 'They're going to call me in an hour to go over our evidence.'

Barnes continued. 'I have been cross-referencing missing persons against the pictures found on Young's wall, which I may add was difficult to look at. I managed to match four of the women from facial analysis, though without DNA samples from CSI, it's impossible to be certain.' He handed four folders to DSI Wright.

Watson smiled. The force had got a good bunch of young up-and-coming officers to nurture and guide over the coming years. French, Sandall, and Barnes were the first to come to the fore. Gone were the days where the force relied on the old boys' brigade to fill the gaps and stifle the young recruits' passage up the ranks. Now the wind of change was blowing through, and Wright was another notch in that change. He shook his head, realising she was talking to him.

'This is going to get horrible,' Wright said, opening the first folder. 'Having to speak to the families of these women to tell them we may know what happened to their loved ones is not something I'm looking forward to. For instance, Viv Miller's family... we cannot even give them peace of mind without a body. That animal Young is the only person who knows where the bodies are.'

Watson glanced at the second name on the list. Caroline Dicks. 'Asking them for something with their DNA on is going to be a wrench.'

'Yes,' Wright said grimly. 'You go back and continue the interview, Terry. We can now place both Samantha Field and Alison Grant at his house and in his van that should be enough.'

A phone rang. Sandall picked it up.

'Boss, DS Monteith is downstairs.' As soon as he had conveyed the message, another phone rang.

'Good, he's safe. I will see what happened last night.' Wright handed the folders back to Barnes and walked to the door with Watson.

Sandall put the phone back down. 'Ma'am. That was the hospital. Samantha Field died twenty minutes ago.'

CHAPTER FOURTEEN

WRIGHT LOOKED WITH PITY at the husk of a man sitting at the other side of her desk. In the space of a few months, this man had been abducted, beaten, and put in an impossible position by both her boss and the biggest crook in Ravenswood. On top of that, his wife had left him, he'd had a fight with one of the Russells' henchmen *and* had been involved in a violent attack against people who'd dissed the crime brothers. Most men would crawl in a corner and call it quits on life with that, but she could see beneath the exterior a light still burning for the job.

'Surely we have enough now to bring them down.' Monteith sounded frustrated.

'We do, but nothing that implicates the Russells directly. We don't want them to walk as soon as we have them. Most of what we have relates to both Lex and Ray, and unfortunately now you. But that bridge we can cross later. We can charge Lex and Ray, but we need something concrete to nail the brothers. What you have found out is great and we can work with it. Just hang in there a few more days. Will either Lex or Ray help us if we offer them something?'

Monteith thought. 'Ray might, but it depends what the offer is. Lex won't. He is becoming a liability. They ask him to do something, and he ends up doing that and a bit more; goes over the top. It's like he feels he can do what he wants under their protection.'

Wright pushed her chair back. 'PC Barnes has been doing extensive digging into both Lex and Ray's background; walk with me and let's see what he has found out.'

They went over to Barnes and asked for the info on the two thugs.

'Alex John Sullivan – born London, son of DI Peter Sullivan of the Met who was arrested together with five colleagues for running a protection racket. Taking a cut from local drug dealers. Any drugs bust, and a handful of money would go missing. He denied everything and claimed they'd set him up. Hung himself in his cell. Little Alex rebelled and got involved in gangs. A couple of minor stints in jail, until he assaulted a policeman with a hammer. Served five years of a ten-year stretch, then disappeared from London.

'Raymond Lucas, local. Went to the same school as the Russells, two years lower. Joined the Army but didn't finish the training. Rumour was that something happened during training, but getting the Army to spill their information is impossible. Started a security business for nightclubs, which he sold. Started working for the Russells soon after, mainly as their driver,' Barnes concluded as he handed the file over.

'Ray said he knew Jimmy and Allan had something on their employees. Maybe this is his secret,' Monteith mused. 'Maybe this will help bring Ray on our side. Lex is a load of dynamite waiting to go off and it could be soon. Ray, on the other hand, plays his cards close to his chest.'

The large metal gates opened, and Ray nudged the Range Rover Evoke through and carried on up the drive to the house, parking in front of the main door. He got out and opened the door for Allan Russell. They stood for a moment on the steps before entering Jimmy Russell's large open-plan house with its fine art and furniture spread throughout.

Allan and Ray made their way through to the vast kitchen-diner which covered the back of the house, overlooking a manicured lawn leading down to the river. A pair of swans passed gracefully by, while a moorhen bobbed along.

'I think this house is my best purchase.' Jimmy, dressed in his suit, was looking out of the bi-folding doors at the garden and the river beyond. Allan and Ray joined him, taking in the grandeur of it all. The dulcet tones of Joe Bonamassa's "India/Mountain Time" seeped into the air through the Bluetooth wall speakers. Jimmy turned to face the two men.

'Right, what the bloody hell happened last night?'

Ray and Allan looked at each other.

'Well?' Jimmy pushed past them and refilled his coffee cup. 'My source at the hospital told me that Don Spedding was admitted to A&E early this morning with a head injury. His wife was hysterical. And the police were there, waiting to interview him.'

'It was Lex,' Ray spat.

'What was Lex? All I said was to give Spedding a warning by leaving the photographs of him and his mistress in the house for his wife to find. What the fuck did Lex do?'

'Spedding came down when they were putting the photos on display. Lex gave him a beating.'

'Why didn't Monteith do anything?' Jimmy was getting angry.

'He was in the kitchen, so he didn't see it, only heard it,' Ray said, siting down at the kitchen island. 'He did follow Lex upstairs when Spedding's wife came down and then fled back up the stairs. Lex was going to give her a going over. Monteith tried to intervene but then left.'

'Where is super copper, by the way?' Jimmy asked, looking pointedly at his watch.

Allan took out his phone out and called Monteith.

'Jimmy, we need to do something about Lex. He's becoming a liability,' Ray said, leaning in close to his boss.

'Yes, I realise,' Jimmy sighed.

Allan finished his call. 'Monteith is on his way to the casino. He's pissed off with Lex after last night. Said Lex went mental while doing a job on Spedding, and he chased his wife upstairs and beat her up.'

Ray looked again at Jimmy.

'I know, I know!' Jimmy said tersely. He walked back towards the open garden doors, coffee cup in hand, with a grim look of determination on his face. A look Allan and Ray had seen many times before.

'What did I miss?' Allan looked confused.

'We were just about to discuss the liability that is Lex,' Ray updated him.

'Oh! And what I just relayed from Monteith did not help,' Allan said, looking at his brother.

'It might have, depends on what Jimmy has planned for him.'

Monteith hastened to the casino. He had little time. At least he knew where everyone was. But where was Lex? Hopefully, still comatosed at home.

Parking round the back, Monteith entered the casino via the staff entrance. He put a smile on his face, trying to act normal, and said 'Hello' and 'Good morning' to the staff. Taking a mug of coffee from the kitchen, he went into the casino. Cleaners were busy tidying, and the bar staff were restocking the shelves. The other security staff did not come in till later in the afternoon, so he knew he did not have them to deal with for a while. Lex was nowhere to be seen.

As he was taking the lift to the floor where the offices were, Monteith knew he only had a small timeframe before the Russells and Ray came back. He started searching for the employees' files. He guessed they'd be in Jimmy Russel's office, but how would he be able to enter it and search without raising suspicion?

Watson exited the interview room after a long interrogation. He hated this part of his job. Catching and bringing in culprits was the easy part. Getting all the evidence lined up with the facts, so the suspects would face trial, was far harder. Young and his heinous crimes left a sour taste in his mouth. *Had the man ever thought about his victims? Considered their feelings?* It made Watson sick.

Roger Young had made them sweat for every ounce of information until Sandall dropped his bombshell. The CPS had given the go-ahead to charge Young with the murders of Samantha Field and Alison Grant.

———

Making sure the coast was clear, Monteith stuck his head around the office door. *Where would Jimmy Russell keep the personnel files? His computer?*

He slipped past the large sofa and chairs to open a door in the far corner. It was locked. He grinned. You don't become a detective without picking up some inside tips. Lock-picking was easy once you knew how to do it.

He removed a small pouch from his pocket containing his Jack Knife multi-tool lock-pick set. Swiftly, he unlocked the door and switched on the light. Before him were ten filing cabinets leaning against three walls in a horseshoe shape.

Monteith knew he had little time left. He quickly skimmed through the filing cabinets until he found the employees' files, ordered alphabetically, at the back of the room. He found Ray's file in the bottom drawer of the cabinet marked A-L. Taking his phone, Monteith snapped pictures of each page before placing the file back. In the next cabinet was the file on Lex and he again took pictures.

His phone pinged. *Bloody Allan again.* He cursed, hands shaking as he checked the message.

Almost there

He cursed again. Feeling the urgency now, he shut the cabinet and made for the door. But something caused him to turn back and re-open it. Inside, he found his own file. What he saw chilled him to the core. His knees turned to jelly, and his head spun. Pulling himself together, he took a photograph of the piece of paper, replaced the file, locked both cabinets, and ensured the cupboard door was shut. As he closed the door to Jimmy's office, he heard the brothers' voices close by.

Sweating profoundly, he nipped into the toilet as they rounded the corner. He splashed cold water on his face and dried it, before walking out of the toilet as casually as he could.

Allan stared at him. 'What have you been up to? Ray here wondered where you had gone last night.' He cast a hard glance at Monteith. 'You don't look well.'

'Upset stomach from the takeaway I had last night,' Monteith lied.

Jimmy and Allan grinned.

'First thing Monday morning, I want to see you in my office,' Jimmy Russell said.

Watson sat in the passenger seat alongside Wright, staring out of the window.

'We need to make sure that what we were told is correct before we talk to Keith,' Wright said, negotiating the city centre's rush-hour traffic, which was becoming a nightmare. 'You knew nothing about this?' She performed a delicate manoeuvre around two cars who had a shunt, leaving the drivers arguing over who was to blame.

'No, of course not. And I'm sure Keith didn't know either. This must be an enormous shock for him.' He paused. 'Besides, do you really think he'd gone to the casino if he'd known? No way.'

They entered the Thelwell estate, passing the sign that read: "Welcome to HELL", and the hostel where a murder victim, Ronald Freeman, had stayed. Watson waved at the manager, Sheila Evans, who was talking to kids in the car park.

'Friends of yours?' Wright smiled.

'Everybody wants to be your friend until they get caught for something.'

The DSI pulled up outside Joseph Clayton's house. Davy's battered Vauxhall Vectra was parked on the drive. As they walked towards the door, it swung open. Davy blocked the entrance with his bulk.

'Hello Davy, is your father in?' Watson asked.

'What the fuck do you want?' Davy folded his arms across his ample chest.

'Got a nice way with words, this one,' Wright commented.

'Don't worry. His bark is worse than his bite.'

'Who's the skirt?' Davy sneered.

'My boss, and her bite is worse than her bark.' Watson drew closer to Davy. 'So, I wouldn't push it. Be a good boy and let us in.'

Davy grumbled and turned his back to them, leaving the door open for them to follow.

'My bite is worse than my bark, is it? I'll remember that,' Wright grinned.

Joseph Clayton appeared from the kitchen as both Wright and Watson came into the front room. He leaned heavily on his cane.

'Mr Watson, how nice to see you.'

'Evening Joseph, sorry to come round unannounced. This is my boss, DSI Wright. Ma'am, this is Joseph Clayton.'

'Enchante,' Joseph said, as he took Wright's hand and kissed it.

'Cut the flannel, Joseph,' Watson joked, as he sat on the sofa next to Wright.

'Manners cost nothing, Mr Watson,' Joseph said as he eased into a chair near the fire, placing the cane within easy reach. 'Davy, tea for everyone, please.'

Davy mumbled something and made his way into the kitchen.

'I take it this is not a social call, and you have opened the envelope?'

'No, it's not, and yes, we have, Mr Clayton.' Wright took a notepad out of her handbag. 'We'd like to know how you learned about Keith Monteith's heritage, providing it's true, of course.'

Joseph stared out of the window. 'Neither of you are from here, are you?'

Both Watson and Wright shook their heads.

'I am local born and bred, so was my father, and his father. The expansion in the 1970s brought people from far and wide, mostly from the south, wanting to escape the cities. But with the moneyed infrastructure and factory work came the crime. I'm not saying it didn't already exist, it's just that with the influx of outsiders, the not-so-savoury sort arrived. The Russells were one of those families.'

Joseph stopped talking as Davy brought in the drinks and set them down on the coffee table. He handed Joseph his cup, which he put on a side table. Davy then sat down on the chair under the window as the old man continued.

'Everybody knew everybody's business before the expansion. You'd be on first-name terms with your local bobbies and knew where they lived, not that there were a lot of them. They knew your business and, providing you kept your nose clean, would leave you alone. In case of turf wars or pub punch-ups, they'd show up, but there weren't many. Until the outsiders came in and tried their luck. The locals wouldn't shit on their own doorsteps.' Joseph stopped and took a swig of his drink.

Wright went to say something, but Watson put his hand on her arm and shook his head. 'Just let him talk. Think of this as a history lesson,' he whispered.

She rolled her eyes but let him continue.

'The Russells arrived in the first wave. Malcolm and Betty, with their sons Jimmy and Allan. They set up home on this estate a couple of streets away. The Monteiths arrived about a month later, Bill and Susan. Susan was pregnant with their firstborn, David.'

Watson looked puzzled. 'I did not know Keith had a brother. He's never mentioned him.'

'You wouldn't,' Joseph said. 'He died when he was two, before Keith was born. Fell over while playing in the garden and cracked his head on the concrete step. Knocked Bill and Susan for six and nearly finished their marriage. Bill wanted to try again for another, but Susan didn't. She withdrew into herself. He started working nights with Preston Trucks just to get out of the house. About a year later, she was pregnant again, but word got around the baby wasn't Bill's.' He stopped and looked at them.

'Malcolm Russell,' Watson exclaimed.

Joseph smiled back.

'Does Keith know?' Wright asked.

'I don't know. Bill and Susan were ecstatic about the pregnancy. Smothered Keith when he was born and covered him in the preverbal cotton wool. He wanted for nothing. You were in the same school year, Mr Watson?'

'Yes.'

Joseph nodded. 'That's right. There were you two, Jimmy and Allan, in the two years above you, and my two below.'

'Did Bill ever learn that Keith was not his?' Wright pressed.

She's thinking about what I'm afraid of. If this is true, Keith was in bigger danger undercover than they'd imagined.

'I believe so. He went to have it out with Malcolm Russell and got beaten up. Like I said, the Russells were not to be messed with even then. Davy found that out at school when he told a teacher about Jimmy's playground sweet scam. Ended up with a broken nose and a cut eye, didn't you?'

Davy laughed. 'It was worth it, as Jimmy got the cane, and he was forced to shut up shop.'

Watson pondered Joseph's motivation. 'After all the years Keith and I have known you, why wait till now to share this with us? Why not earlier?'

Joseph looked at them all in turn. 'Lung cancer,' he said drily. 'Docs have given me three months at most.'

Watson looked at Davy.

'It's true,' Davy said. 'Dad's not been well for a bit. He did not want any fuss and with his age, he refused treatment.'

Wright and Watson took their leave soon after. He was still in shock. Monteith the half-brother to the biggest crooks in the city. It did not matter if he had known about it or not, he *had* to be pulled out. Could he bring down the criminal brothers' empire before?

———

Katie Monteith settled down in front of the television with her mother, after she'd tucked in Rebecca and Pixie in bed for the night. Her mind still whirred from her husband's visit, when he'd revealed her the truth about his undercover work.

Her mother came in with two cups of tea, handing her one before taking a seat in a chair.

'Have you decided what you're going to do?'

'Uh, what? No. Yes. Oh, I don't know. Stop asking me, Mum. I haven't a clue what day it is, never mind anything else, especially with this headache.' She got up and went into the kitchen to the medicine cabinet. Taking two paracetamol, she swallowed them down with some water before re-entering the living room. *Another interrogation,* she thought bitterly. A routine they played out most nights. Mother started with both barrels even before Katie had time to sit down.

'You were all set to divorce that thing you call a husband until he came round with that sob story. I can see you have fallen for it, hook, line, and sinker.'

'His name is KEITH, in case you've forgotten,' Katie yelled. 'He is the father of your two grandchildren, who are upstairs right now.'

'The only thing he has done right is produce two lovely children. Your marriage has been in a shambles from the start.' Her barbed vicious comment wounded Katie, but didn't surprise her.

'How many more times are you going to believe what he says about giving up gambling? He's an addict and always will be. Gambled your money away so you could not go on that holiday to Spain. Had his car attacked and so much debt owed to the biggest crooks in the city.'

Katie looked surprised.

Her mother grumbled, 'Hey, I'm not just a doddery old widow living on her own, I know what goes on. Word gets about. We don't talk about knitting patterns and baking cakes at the community centre, you know. So, what cock-and-bull story has he come up with this time?'

Katie sighed. She couldn't stop the tears from falling as she told her mother what Keith had said.

Her mother sat unmoved throughout it all.

A truce was declared about 10 o'clock.

When Katie went to bed an hour later, she found Rebecca sitting at the top of the stairs.

'Have you been arguing over dad again?'

Katie could see that Rebecca had been crying. *Poor thing, she must have overheard everything.*

She coaxed her daughter back to the bedroom and lay beside her. They both drifted off to sleep.

Monteith stared at the CCTV monitors in front of him, his mind elsewhere. Friday nights and the weekends were the busiest, and tonight was no exception. The casino floor was rammed full of punters handing over their hard-earned cash to the Russell brothers. More customers meant more trouble. The security guards downstairs had already thrown out five drunks who didn't know when to quit chatting up the female bar staff or try to kick and punch the fruit machines after having lost all their money. To top it off, one player had been caught counting the cards during a game of blackjack. He had been chucked on the streets without his money.

His phone beeped. A text message from Watson.

> Need to see you. Urgent. BBQ at my place tomorrow at 12 p.m. Everyone will be there. Bring Katie and the girls.

He dropped his phone back into his pocket and looked down on the Russell brothers shaking hands with the rich, infamous and corrupt by the restaurant and felt sick. Ray had told him why they had visited Don Spedding. At least the council had the balls to stand up against them for once, even though Spedding had ended up in hospital. The thought of the Russells' Gentleman's Club, where they could fleece their clients and use the video recordings as blackmail was abhorrent. But what turned his stomach was the knowledge that he might be related to them, according to what he'd read in his file. *Why had no-one told him?* And how could he broach the subject with the Russells? He couldn't exactly ask them, could he? 'Hey, I just found out I'm your half-brother.'

Not without divulging how he'd discovered the information.

CHAPTER FIFTEEN

Saturday Noon

THE HEAT WAS BUILDING as Monteith walked up the drive to Watson's front door. He recognised both his and Sally's cars, but the other two parked on the road outside were new to him. As he knocked, Sally opened the door wide.

'Hello, stranger,' she said. He kissed her on the cheek and gave her a hug. 'No Katie and the girls?'

'No. I asked Katie if she wanted to come, but no deal. Things are still very fragile between the two of us. She did ask if you could meet her next week, though.'

'I will give her a ring tomorrow,' Sally promised, as she closed the door. 'Go through to the kitchen. Everyone's in there.'

Monteith entered the kitchen and stopped in the doorway. Watson stood there in his Meatloaf T-shirt, but the other two guests caught him off guard. DSI Wright in a floral dress and Chief Superintendent Matthews in a crisp shirt, tie, and blazer.

'Hi, feller. What's your poison?' Watson asked, grinning widely.

'A beer please,' he replied, nodding to Wright and Matthews.

'Good to see you,' Matthews said, as he put his hand out. Monteith shook it, looking confused. Matthews noticed. 'Don't worry Keith. We wanted to see how you were coping.' Turning to Watson, he nodded. 'Your office?'

Watson handed him a bottle of San Miguel and winked before opening the door. They all traipsed in, with Watson sitting down at his computer. Matthews shut the door. Wright and Monteith sat on two wooden chairs next to each other.

Wright started, 'Sorry to hoodwink you Keith, something has come to light that we thought you should know about. Which is why we are meeting here and not at work because we don't want this to go around the station.'

Monteith hesitated, then said, 'I wanted to speak to you as well. Things have gone on this week and I'm at a greater risk of being discovered every day. I know they are testing my allegiance, but I am getting worried about my safety.'

'Thanks to your information-gathering, up till now we were building an excellent evidence file to bring the Russell empire to an end. We have also received other information from a source which will help us, but there is something that could jeopardise what we've garnered.'

'Okay...?'

Watson opened a drawer in his desk, pulled out an envelope and handed it to Wright. She opened it and took out the papers.

'This information has stayed just between us three and Joseph Clayton who gave it to us, and that's where we want to keep it.' Wright looked at Monteith, who nodded.

Wright handed the two sheets over to Monteith. He scanned the first sheet, then continued on the second.

Keith Monteith is Jimmy and Allan Russell's half-brother

He glanced up. 'Where did you say you got this from?'

'Joseph Clayton gave it to me,' Watson said. 'That piece of paper is photo-copied from a book with listings of all the things the Russells and their dad have been involved in.'

'Is there any truth in it?' Wright took over.

"You said you got this from Joseph Clayton?" Monteith asked, looking around the room.

'Yes,' Wright confirmed.

Monteith looked beaten. 'Before yesterday, I would have said it was a lie and totally bonkers. Me related to the Russells! Whoever said it would be on the other end of battering - and that included Joseph bloody Clayton.' He reached inside his jacket and removed his phone. Handing it across to Watson, he asked him to download the photos he had taken.

There was a knock on the door.

'Yes?'

'Just to let you know that our other guests are arriving, and are wondering where you are,' Sally said.

'Thanks, love, we won't be much longer,' Watson called out, as he started downloading the photographs.

Monteith continued, 'Yesterday, while the Russells and their goons were out, I took the chance to do some "research" in the employees' files. On my phone are some pictures I snapped from Lex

159

and Ray's files.' He took a swig of his beer. 'Also on there are photos of what the Russells had on my file. One of them is of what looks like a copy of an official statement by Malcolm Russell, acknowledging he is my father. I have never seen this before, so I don't know if it's genuine. My birth certificate has both my parents on it, God rest their souls.'

Watson finished downloading and looked at some of them with Matthews.

'Good work Keith,' Matthews said. 'This is a great help. Terry, can you email them across to yours, mine and Tanya's computers so we can work on them next week? Also, make a CD as a backup, then delete them from this computer.'

'Yes, sir.'

Matthews turned to Monteith. 'Tanya told me what happened the other night. That you wanted to be pulled out. It that still the case?'

Monteith shook his head vehemently. 'I'm staying till the end. Don't pull me out now. I want to bring the bastards down even more. Let's crucify them.'

The Saturday afternoon sun glinted off the surface of the river, with the branches from the overhanging bushes dipping into the water, as if they were drinking from it.

Up on the patio, Jimmy Russell sat looking through his binoculars at the birds floating by. Even more so to check out the house across the river. Concentrating on the wife of the family who sunbathed topless on days like this. Today she was naked. She knew he was watching her and gave Jimmy a good view of her tanned body.

A body Jimmy knew every inch of; they had been seeing each other for six months now. Her husband worked abroad in banking for two weeks each month. Jimmy had got to know them after they had dined at his restaurant with some foreign guests.

'Admiring the view again?' Allan stood by his brother, shielding his eyes from the sun's glare.

'I never thought birdwatching was such a great hobby,' Jimmy replied, gazing longingly at the woman's full-frontal plumage.

'Bollocks. You used to stare at Diane Butcher across the road when you were fifteen with a small set of binoculars,' Allan reminded Jimmy as he poured himself a coffee.

'I didn't hear you telling me off. You got an eyeful as well, if I remember rightly.'

'Well, watching her get changed was better than watching television.'

Jimmy could not remember how many women he had bedded over the years. Diane Butcher the first: his seventeenth birthday present. Their late father, Malcolm, had also been a womaniser. Their mother, Betty, did nothing to stop him; if she had tried, he would get violent. Jimmy had followed in his footsteps.

'We need to restructure and be more forceful with those against us. We are getting slack and becoming soft with people,' Jimmy commented, looking down at the iPad in his hand.

'Well, Don Spedding certainly got the message,' Allan reminded him.

'I'm not talking about business interests. They look after themselves once we put some pressure on. Don was a pain in the arse who could not do his job properly.'

'What are you on about, Jimmy? A restructure of what?'

'Brother, we need to test the loyalty of those around us. Tommy Burke wasn't, so we had to get rid of him. There are several others who also need to be relieved of their duty. Promote some others who have shown backbone.'

'Got anybody in mind?'

'The bar takings have been down over the last two weeks, so I put a camera out the back.' Jimmy handed the iPad to Allan, so that he could see the footage on the screen.

'Interesting. When are they working next?'

'Their last shift will be tonight, and it will definitely be their last.'

Allan nodded. 'Who else have you got your eye on?'

'A few. Lex, Keith, and Ray, we need to redistribute their roles. Keith is wasted sat in that office every night. Bruce can do his job, free Keith up to do more important stuff.'

Before Allan could press his brother on what he had planned, Ray came strolling out.

Jimmy got up and said, 'We'll discuss it later, at the casino,' then patted Allan on the shoulder. 'It will be worth it, I promise you, dear brother.'

Sunday Morning

Watson's BBQ alcohol-induced headache had not subsided by the time Simon's game had kicked off. It was a relegation grudge match

Ryland U14 v Normanton U14. Winner stayed up, loser went down. A draw and Ryland survive.

The manager, Nick Thomas, told Watson that the manager of Ravenswood Rovers' U14 was watching from a distance so as not to put pressure on Simon and teammate Lance Brewster. Nick nodded towards a smartly dressed man standing on the grass behind a goalpost.

Sally, Jason, and Rachael had come along to cheer Simon on. Sally took Rachael to the play area before the match started, leaving Watson and Jason on the touchline, talking to the other parents. A group of teenage boys and girls dressed in tracksuits were gathering across the park and started stretching. Their trainer called them over and set them off on a run.

Both teams took up their positions. The match was about to start and Sally and Rachael joined Watson, who was looking at the manager from Ravenswood Rovers, who was making notes on an iPad.

The first fifteen minutes were littered with mistakes by both teams. *Nerves*, Watson smiled. He glanced at the Ravenswood Rovers manager, who hadn't moved at all. Further away were the teenage runners who'd just finished their first sprint and were stopping for a break. The trainer was going around speaking to them and it set Watson's police antenna on alert. It was the trainer's demeanour around the girls, getting close to them as he talked and occasionally touching them. A hand on the shoulder here, a light stroke on the arm there.

Sally nudged Watson in time for him to see Normanton take the lead. Ryland did not clear the ball from a corner and it was bundled in by a Normanton player. The Ryland players started arguing between themselves while the Normanton players ran off, celebrating. Simon encouraged his teammates to get their minds back on the game, which eventually did.

The difference in the two sides at half-time was poles apart. Normanton's players were hyped up and buzzing. Their manager was as excited as if they had already won the match. Their parents, too, seemed pleased. On the other side of the pitch, Nick stood in front of the Ryland players, who sat on the ground, listening to his pep-talk.

The manager of Ravenswood Rovers' U14s had left his viewpoint and had joined the crowd on the sidelines.

Coming back from the tea bar, Watson spotted a man he recognised. Excusing himself from Sally, he wandered over to the man.

'Morning Jeff.' Jeff Johnson, the county police force detective. 'What brings you onto our patch?'

After shaking hands, Jeff nodded his head toward the athletics trainer. 'As you know, we have been following Ian Fellows for some time. We have corroborative evidence of his behaviour towards the female runners at the club.'

'We were going to have a word with him regarding a case we have just closed.'

'The Alison Grant and Samantha Field one. Yes, good work getting Roger Young. Where did Fellows fit in?'

'Alison was being trained by Fellows, and her boyfriend told us about his behaviour. Also, Steph Parkinson said she quit the club because of him.'

'We interviewed Steph Parkinson the other day with her father. Very interesting what she said. So much so, we are picking him up this morning. That's Fellows' car.' Jeff pointed to a Skoda Octavia parked just down the row. 'We have been videoing his training this morning for more evidence. We should be done before your football match is finished.'

'I will watch the fireworks then.' Watson shook hands with Jeff and made his way back to Sally.

The second half began with both teams vying for the upper hand. The Ryland team did so in just seven minutes in. Simon received the ball and placed a pinpoint ball to their striker, ran it through the Normanton defence, taking his time to draw the keeper out. He slipped the ball under him and into the net. Goal!

The Ryland team jumped on the striker in elation, the parents cheered on the sideline. Cheers and glee-filled shouts of encouragement filled the field.

'Good through-pass from your lad.' Watson turned to find the Ravenswood Rovers manager standing beside him. 'I'm Thomas Park.'

'Terry Watson. And thanks,' Watson introduced himself. He kept his eye on both the match and Fellows as they spoke. The training session ended halfway through the second half of the match. Fellows packed up his stuff and made his way back to his car, his arm around the shoulder of a girl as he crossed the field.

Watson stood back from the crowd, holding the man in his sight from the car park. As Fellows dropped his equipment into the boot of his car, Jeff and his partner walked over to him. A squad car turned the corner, blocking his car in. Fellows tried to make a run for it but was caught, handcuffed, and put in the back of the squad car. A crowd had gathered watching Fellows being driven away. Jeff looked up as he opened his car door and waved at Watson before he got in.

The match became a battle of attrition. Both teams refusing to give an inch in their determination to avoid relegation. Ryland had the upper hand by drawing, Normanton had to score but were coming up against a Lance Brewster-led defence.

With three minutes to go, Ryland's winger was brought down for a free kick near the right-hand side of the Normanton penalty area. The free kick was swung over into the mass of players in the penalty area. A, a Normanton defender got his head to the ball, sending it out to the edge of the front and centre area where Simon was standing. Everything seemed to go into slow motion as Simon took aim. He struck the ball skillfully with his right foot, watching it arrow through the players in front of him, glancing off the inside of the post and nestling in the top corner of the net.

It took everyone a couple of seconds to register what had just happened. Then euphoria exploded. The Ryland players shot off after Simon, who was wheeling away after the goal towards his parents, arm outstretched like an Alan Shearer goal celebration..

He was at the halfway line before his teammates caught up and jumped on him. Some of the Normanton players collapsed in tears, while others pleaded with the referee to disallow the goal.

Sally jumped into Watson's arms. Jason and Rachael were running around screaming in delight. Thomas Park wore a huge smile on his face, making notes.

The final whistle followed soon after. Rylands had survived. Players and parents ran to each other to celebrate. Nick Thomas walked over to the Normanton manager to shake hands before running over to join in the celebrations.

Watson could feel his headache returning with all the celebrating and shouting. He smiled. It was worth it.

CHAPTER SIXTEEN

Monday 6 a.m.

EARLY MORNING RAIDS WERE part and parcel of the job. WPC Dawn Raid as they were colloquially known in the past.

Sandall and Lorimer were with Watson in his car. He was ready to issue the order "go". The ARU were in position as the three of them alighted from the car.

Lorimer signalled to the lead officer. What followed was the sound of the door caving in under the impact of the enforcer.

'POLICE! POLICE!' echoed down the hallway of the terraced house. Armed officers entered the property, splitting in groups of two to cover both floors. The downstairs rooms were given the all-clear as Watson and Lorimer headed upstairs where they found their suspect. He was swearing profoundly, lying on the bedroom floor as two burly officers were cuffing him.

His female companion was trying to cover up her naked body on the bed. The young woman looked no older than seventeen.

The officers managed to pull him upright just as Watson entered the bedroom. 'Get a female officer in here and give the young lady some clothes. She can come with us as well,' he ordered.

Watson stood in front of the man they had come for. 'Alex John Sullivan you are under arrest for the murder of Wayne Marsh. He continued to read Lex his rights under a torrent of abuse. 'Get him dressed.' Watson finished, before turning and going back downstairs to find Sandall in the front room.

'I want this place given a thorough going through. If you find anything related to the Russells, bag it. We need to make sure we have done our job properly; we cannot leave a single stone unturned.'

'Yes sir,' Sandall nodded.

Watson came back out into the hall as Lex was brought downstairs, dressed in a tracksuit. 'You bastard. I know where you live and I'm coming after your family. You're a dead man.'

'I've heard it all before Lex. It'll be a long time before you see the outside again. Get him out of here,' Watson said curtly.

Monteith sat down on the green leather sofa in Jimmy Russell's office. Jimmy and Allan were in the two leather chairs on the other side of the large glass coffee table. Both with open files on their laps and a notebook resting on a large arm rest of their chair.

'Keith,' Jimmy started, 'you have been with us for almost two months. We just wanted a chat to see how you are doing.'

Monteith's mind went into overdrive. This didn't sound like the Jimmy Russell he knew.

'Erm, it's going okay apart from having been abducted, being forced to give up my career in the force–'

Jimmy put his hand up. 'We went through all that with you when you came to work for us.'

'Made to work for you!' Monteith snapped.

Jimmy looked up from the file on his knee, 'Nobody made you come here; we just pointed out the ramifications if you didn't.'

Monteith shot up, anger written on his face.

'SIT DOWN, I've not finished!' Jimmy's voice was as hard as his stare.

Monteith shot glances at both the brothers before slowly sitting back down.

Jimmy continued, 'The reason we asked you to come in is that we are planning to expand the business. We'd like you to help us.'

Monteith waited for the punchline. *Restructure and expansion – interesting.*

Jimmy looked at Allan, who took a paper from his file and slid it across the table towards Monteith. 'We want you to run the business with us.'

Monteith looked at them both. *What the hell?* He picked up the paper, a contract ready for him to sign. Ready for him to become a partner in the Russells' business empire.

'Why me? Why not Lex, Ray or anyone else?'

Both brothers snorted. 'You're family.'

'No, I'm not.'

Jimmy looked directly at Monteith, 'You are our half-brother whether you like it or not. The birth certificate in your possession might say different but we have an official statement signed by our father saying otherwise. We share the same biological father. You didn't think we paid you all this attention for no reason.'

Well, there it is. Now to act dumb. Let's hope they believe me.

'Why do you think we tried to help you when your gambling got out of hand?' Jimmy asked. 'We *had* to punish you. We saw how out of hand it was getting and had to do something about it. Banning you from the tables and getting you to repay your debts was the only course of action, brother.'

Something was niggling Monteith.

'Why this statement? Why wasn't I told who my father was?'

'Honestly? I don't know.' Jimmy shrugged. 'I remember when I was about six your father having a big row with our dad.'

The door flew open. Ray stumbled into the room. 'Boss.'

'Can't you see we are in a meeting?' Jimmy shouted.

'Sorry, but Lex has been arrested. I went to pick him up, and the road was sealed off with police. Spoke to someone who said there was an early morning raid and Lex had been carted off, along with a young woman.'

'Fucking jerk! Can't he keep it in his pants?' Jimmy jumped up from his chair.

Monteith found it hard to keep a smile off his face. *One down, three to go.*

Jimmy turned back to Monteith. 'Right. Time you started earning your way as a partner in this business. Do you have any contacts in the force you can trust?'

Ray looked at Monteith in surprise.

Monteith mouthed, 'I'll tell you later.' Out loud, he said, 'I burned a lot of bridges working for you. Most of them still want my guts for garters, they certainly are no longer talking to me. Why?'

'Find out, by whatever means necessary, why Lex has been arrested, and what's he has been saying. We need to cover our arses in case he turns snitch. Ray, you go with him.'

The alarm sounded from the interview room, bringing every officer available to the assistance of DCI Watson and DS Lorimer. Four officers came flying through the door where Lex could be seen, holding his solicitor by the collar up against the wall. It took all of them to grapple him off the man and re-cuff him.

'Are you alright?' Watson asked the solicitor, Colin Roberts, after the officers had marched Lex back to his cell.

'Yes. I think so. Don't think he wants to co-operate with any of us,' Roberts replied, stuffing his paperwork back in his bag. 'I will speak to him when he has calmed down. Hopefully, he will see sense.'

'It's sense he seems to be lacking in the first place... Good luck with that,' Watson commented.

He made his way towards the office with Lorimer.

'That was quick,' Wright said, looking at her watch.

'Lex attacked his solicitor before the interview could begin,' Watson explained.

'It's his time he is wasting, not ours. With the footage we have of Lex forcing the tablets down Wayne Marsh's throat and the CCTV footage of him dumping Wayne's body in the park, CPS have already given us the go-ahead to charge him.'

Watson's mobile phone rang as Wright followed him into his office. It was Monteith.

'News of Lex's arrest has made it back to base, and they're not happy. How's the interrogation going?'

'Apart from him attacking his solicitor, it's not started.'

'That's good then,' Monteith laughed. 'Can you start phase two now? Repeat, now.'

Watson repeated the words to Wright who nodded her go-ahead. 'Meet you at the place.'

Monteith put his phone away, flushed the toilet and washed his hands, before making his way to his car.

'All good?' Ray asked as he got in.

'Yep.'

'How long have you worked for Jimmy and Allan?' Monteith asked, as he pulled into traffic, heading for the city centre. He knew he had to probe to get Ray to talk. He was the quiet one, taking everything in, not saying much unless asked to comment. When he opened his mouth, it was always worth listening to. A great right-hand man for the Russells and a coup if they could get him to turn.

Ray puffed out his cheeks. 'About five or six years, I think. Started in security, like you.'

'It that your forte? What you did before?'

'Yes, had my own company after coming out of the army. Sold it when the regulations got too tight, cost too much to keep it viable with all the red tape.'

Monteith eased out of the traffic and took the turning towards Copeland.

'So, what has Jimmy Russell got on you?' He glanced at Ray. 'You know mine is my gambling, and Lex's is probably something from his time in London. What's yours?'

Ray looked at Monteith, then back out of the windscreen. 'There was a fight at a local nightclub where I was working on security. A well-known drug dealer died. Jimmy killed him. I saw him do it. He said I would end up the same way if I told the old bill. When the police arrived, I gave them a false description of the culprit. Then when I sold the company, Jimmy gave me a job.'

'So, he bought your silence.'

Ray didn't reply.

Monteith swung his car into an industrial estate and parked behind Watson's Ford Focus.

'We're here,' he said, as they both watched Watson walk over and get into the back of Monteith's BMW.

'You know if I'm seen speaking to you, I'm done for. They're going to kill me. Your name has been banned back at the station,' Watson said angrily. He pointed to Ray. 'Who the fuck is this?'

'Don't get on your high horse. You didn't have to see me; you could have told me to fuck off like the rest of them. Anyway, this is Ray, works for the Russells as their right-hand man. They told him to come to make sure I didn't do a runner.'

'Hello Ray, you're under arrest,' Watson replied, flashing his ID card.

'Fuck off,' Ray spat. 'You bastard Keith.' He opened the door and got halfway out, straight into the grip of DS Lorimer and DC French who spun him round and pushed him against the side of the car, grabbing his wrists to cuff him. Lorimer cautioned him, before handing him to a uniformed constable who would drive him to the custody suite.

'If you've dented my car, you will pay,' Monteith shouted through the open door.

Lorimer lent in, smiling. 'Add it to Ray's charge sheet.'

———

DSI Wright stood in the CCTV room, looking at the video feeds from the two interview rooms. The first one contained Ray and his solicitor; the second had Lex, now he had calmed down, with his solicitor.

The doors to both rooms opened at the same time. Watson and Sandall for Lex, Lorimer and French for Ray. Both interviews started with an introduction for the benefit of the recording equipment. When Lex was told that the interview was being videoed, he stuck his middle finger up to the camera. Both men were told that they would benefit from giving up Jimmy and Allan.

Watson had considered bringing in Monteith to interview Ray, but he had decided against it. Not yet, anyway. It would also be far too dangerous to let Monteith go back to the Russells on his own; Monteith, therefore, was back where he belonged.

'Lex,' Watson started the interview, 'do you know of a man named Wayne Marsh?'

'You know I do,' Lex replied, relaxing in his chair, arms folded. His solicitor had informed him prior to the preliminary introductions following his caution that if he pulled any more crap he'd be on his own. He was behaving. So far.

'How do you know Wayne Marsh?'

'He was hanging around the casino selling drugs,' Lex said impassively.

Watson opened the file on the table in front of him and brought out a photo. 'I am showing Lex Sullivan evidence number AS1. 'Who is this a photograph of?'

'Wayne Marsh.'

'Mr Marsh died shortly after this image was captured on one of the cameras inside the casino. Do you know anything about his death?'

Lex looked at his solicitor. Leaning over, he said, 'Yes, I killed Wayne Marsh – but I was ordered to do so.'

Watson cast a glance at Sandall before going back to Lex. 'Who instructed you to murder Wayne Marsh?'

Lex looked again at his solicitor, who nodded. 'Allan Russell.'

'What exactly did he say to you?'

'He said: "you know what to do" and handed me the bags of ecstasy we had taken from Wayne.'

'What did you assume?'

'That he wanted me to get rid of Wayne by giving him the ecstasy.'

'Feeding him the pills?'

'Yes.'

Monteith's phone rang as he came to stand beside DSI Wright, watching the developments from both interviews, knowing they just had been given a foot into the door to bring down the Russells. He scanned the number on the screen.

'Jimmy Russell, wondering what is happening, I expect.'

Wright grinned. 'Let him sweat. We have eyes on him. He's not going anywhere.'

CHAPTER SEVENTEEN

'ANSWER THE FUCKING PHONE,' Jimmy shouted at his mobile, slamming it down on his desk. 'Where the hell are they? How long does it take to get information?' He shot a look at Allan, standing by the desk. 'I don't like this. Lex gets arrested and now we cannot get hold of Keith or Ray.'

Their father, Malcolm, had installed the need to be in control in his sons. Make sure you are in control of everything you do, especially in business. Make people know who is in charge. Now Jimmy didn't feel in control or in charge. He went and poured a stiff drink, showing the decanter to Allan, who shook his head.

'His phone might just be out of range,' Allan said calmly.

'What, Ray's too?'

'No, you're right. It's iffy.'

'Iffy?' Jimmy repeated, incredulously. 'It fucking stinks. Things have got slack around here. Was I right to bring Lex and Keith into the business?'

'Brother, you have always done what was necessary. Lex was brought in as a back-up to the security when it was needed. He thinks he can do whatever he wants, protected by you. Maybe it is time to get rid of him now he's been arrested. Whatever he says, we can deny it and say we knew nothing about it. He is on his own now.

Keith, on the other hand, is our half-brother. You have kept an eye on him since we knew. Ok, he went to the dark side, and he joined the police, but look how he has ended up. You have saved him, stopped him gambling, brought him back from the dark side and into the family fold. He will be an asset to the business. He's done his apprenticeship by being Chief of Security and he has done it well. Now it's time he stepped up and joined us at the top of the business. Let him run this place, and we can concentrate on other projects.'

—

During a break in the interviews, the team gathered in the office for a brief on the imminent arrest of the Russell brothers.

Chief Superintendent Matthews had joined them.

'We have enough to arrest them. I am going to be a marked man if we don't go in now.' Monteith was pacing around the office like a caged animal.

'I understand your frustration, DS Monteith, and we will get them when we have everything in order,' said Matthews.

'Well, what have we got? Surely it's enough,' Monteith exclaimed. 'With what I have given you together with what Joseph Clayton has. Let's get on with it.'

'Calm down, Keith,' Wright intervened. She turned to Gary Barnes. 'Have you got the up-to-date list of what we have on the Russells?'

Barnes handed her the file. She read, 'We have Allan for ordering the murder of drug dealer Wayne Marsh. Off Joseph Clayton's list, I have confirmation of a cold case Allan was involved in. A derelict building which the Russells were after was torched. Squatters had moved in and two of them died. For Jimmy, we have ordering the abduction of DS Monteith. Ordering the attack on council worker Don Spedding, as well as the attack on their previous Chief of Security, Tommy Burke. I have confirmed that a drug dealer by the name of Jason King, also known as Big K, was killed at a nightclub where Ray handled the security. Ray admitted he covered up for Jimmy, who murdered the man.'

Smiles broke out over everybody's faces.

'And we have both Lex and Ray tweeting like birds,' Watson added.

All eyes were squarely on Matthews, waiting for his decision. He frowned, was silent. Then he sighed and said, 'Time to finish this. Bring them in.'

The room erupted in cheers. At last, they were could bring down the biggest crooks in the city. A pair of criminal brothers daring anybody to challenge them; those that defied them were destroyed. This time they got them.

The convoy made its way out of the city centre towards the Russells' casino. DCI Watson and DS Monteith in the lead car, with DS Lorimer, DC Sandall, and DC French in the next. Behind them PC Barnes and their ARU friends, in a marked Ford Transit.

'Good to have you back,' Watson said, glancing at Monteith.

'Missed me then?' Monteith grinned.

'Erm no. Just saying it's good to have you back.'

'Liar.'

'Well, just a bit then.'

They looked at each other and started laughing.

Monteith's phone rang. 'Jimmy Russell again.'

'Tell him you are on your way. It's the truth, just not with Ray.'

'Finally, they're on their way back,' Jimmy said, sliding his phone into his pocket. The brothers had made their way down to the casino floor to welcome their visitor.

'Mr Grant, thank you for coming at short notice.' Jimmy held out his hand to David Grant.

'Mr Russell, It's me who should thank you, and your brother of course,' Grant replied, shaking his hand. 'Your interest in financing my company is overwhelming.'

'Please take a seat.' Jimmy directed their visitor to the lounge inside the bar.

Once they were settled, and both had drinks in front of them, Jimmy continued. 'First, my condolences on the loss of your daughter. I read about it in the paper. When is the funeral?'

Grant swallowed. 'Thank you. It's next week.'

'Please send us the bill. We'd be only too glad to cover the cost.'

David Grant choked back tears. 'I couldn't let you do that.'

'It's the least we can do for a business partner.'

'Thank you, sir,' Grant whispered.

'Mr Grant, we've given it a lot of thought, and we feel that Argent Logistics could do with our help. We have been looking to expand into logistics and distribution for some time and your company would be the perfect way to start. Using your experience in the field and our money and contacts to back it, we can expand your enterprise to the next level.'

Allan smiled inwardly, watching his brother in action. Negotiating was his forte. He reached into a file and brought out a raft of paperwork, which he placed on the table in front of David Grant. 'Please survey the contract we have had written up and, if you are happy, sign here, here and here,' he indicated.

'I wouldn't sign that contract if I were you, Mr Grant,' Watson bellowed from the end of the room as he and Monteith walked across the floor towards the table, closely followed by Lorimer, Sandall, and French. They had come in through the staff entrance. PC Barnes and the other uniforms were guarding all the exits.

'What the fuck has it got to do with you?' Grant exploded.

Jimmy and Allan stood in front of the two plain-clothed detectives, the rage visibly building on their faces. 'Keith, what the hell is going on? Where is Ray?'

Both Monteith and Watson produced their ID cards, Monteith indicating to Watson with a tilt of his head that he was going to do the honours. 'Ray and Lex are back at the station helping us with our inquiries. Jimmy and Allan Russell, you are both under arrest.'

Grant shot up out of his seat and launched himself at Watson. 'You couldn't stop my daughter from being killed, now you want to ruin my business!' He balled his fist and punched him on the arm. Watson swayed out of the way.

Lorimer and Sandall grabbed Grant and dragged him to the floor, cuffing him. 'I am arresting you for assaulting a police officer.'

Grant cursed as he was handed over to uniform, threatening to take Watson's badge off him. Jimmy and Allan took advantage of the distraction and made a run for the rear exit, but were caught in the doorway by the officers standing on guard. They doubled back and headed into the restaurant, dodging cleaners and other personnel.

Monteith led the chase after them, closely followed by the rest of the detectives.

Jimmy and Allan threw chairs to block their pursuing officers and detoured into the kitchen, only to come face to face with two more police officers. Picking up a carving knife and a boning knife the two turned back into the restaurant.

Watson and Monteith cornered them.

'Why are you running? We only want to ask you a few questions back at the station.' Monteith said sarcastically.

'You lied to us, Keith,' Jimmy said.

'I never left the force. I wouldn't come and work for you in your wildest dreams. Jimmy and Allan Russell, I am arresting you for the abduction of a serving police officer, and that's just for starters.'

'Whatever Lex and Ray have told you, it's not true,' Allan said.

'Who said they told us anything? We don't need them to verify that you arranged my abduction; we have them on camera, stuffing me into the van. We've got you, Allan, pulling out of the car park opposite and following the van. We don't need Lex or Ray to help put you away.'

Watson put a hand on Monteith's arm. 'Calm down, take a walk out of here.' He nodded back towards the main exit. Monteith glared at the brothers before turning away.

It was Watson's turn to glare at the Russells. Lorimer, Sandall, and French stood behind him. 'I'm sorry, my partner has been under a lot of stress. And as he said, you are both under arrest for abduction. Now, are you going to drop the knives and accompany us to the station?'

Jimmy and Allan looked at their knives and each other. They smiled grimly.

Three Weeks Later

Watson wandered into the office, his arm still in a sling following the takedown of the Russell brothers. Jimmy had managed to get a swing in with his knife before being tasered, hitting Watson in the upper arm. Allan had been tasered before he'd been able to get a blow in.

He took a seat in DSI Wright's office. He had been called in for a back to work debrief.

'How are you feeling, Terry?' Wright asked, as she put a coffee cup down for him and sat down.

'I feel fine, ready to return to work. The arm is still a bit sore and the stitches are due out at the end of the week. Just need your say-so.'

Wright looked at her computer and pressed a few keys. 'Before you can return, you are to see a force approved counsellor and it will be their say on when you will be allowed back. I would love to see you behind your desk tomorrow, but I must follow protocol. And with everything you have suffered over the last few months, means the powers that be upstairs have decreed you consult a therapist before starting back.'

Watson grimaced.

Wright passed him the details, adding, 'He is expecting you this afternoon.'

—

The list of charges against the Russell brothers, Lex, and Ray became lengthy once word of their arrest got out. The fraud office opened up a number of lines of inquiries against their activities, interviewing present and former employees of the businesses the Russells were involved in.

Jimmy Russell had been charged with the murder of Jason King. Allan was charged with the murder of the two squatters from the building fire, also with the murder of Wayne Marsh, along with Lex. All were charged with the abduction of Monteith and the holding of Monteith against his will. Various ABH and GBH charges were issued against all of them, including the assaults on Don Spedding and Tommy Burke.

Wright, Monteith, and Matthews were in court to hear Jimmy, Allan, Lex and Ray say 'NOT GUILTY' to all charges against them. Their smiles were wiped off their faces when bail was denied. The judge agreed with the police, naming flight risk and witness intimidation as reasons they should be kept behind bars.

—

Roger Young had been charged with the murders of Alison Grant and Samantha Field, and with bail denied, they continued to interview him in prison. The bodies of Viv Miller and Caroline Dicks were found buried behind Young's farmhouse, in a field he had sold to his neighbouring farm, bringing the number of charges to four. They were convinced he had taken more young women and butchered them.

During an interview with newly promoted Detective Inspector Monteith and Detective Constable Sandall, Young had divulged the whereabouts of two more women he'd murdered.

'I will tell you where Stacey Kitchen and Angela Perry are, but you won't be able to get to the bodies,' Young chuckled. 'I was putting up fences in a village south of here when I came across them. Baxley, I think the place was.' Young leaned back in his chair, looking like he didn't have a care in the world. 'There was a new estate being built across from where I was working. They are buried somewhere on that estate, but you won't find them.'

Monteith and Sandall looked at each other. 'Why is that?' Sandall finally asked.

Young lent forward, arms on the table. Staring straight at the two detectives, 'Because when I buried them, it was dark. Their bodies are beneath two houses, put there before the concrete had been poured into the foundations. Now the estate has been completed, with families living there.' He burst out laughing and turned to the prison guard standing in the corner of the room. 'I'm finished; take me back to my cell.'

THE END

To be continued in book 3 of the Ravenswood Crime Series:
Battle Lines

BATTLE LINES

PROLOGUE

TRAPPED AND STRUGGLING TO break loose from the bands that tied his arms and legs, he screamed out for help.

None came.

He had been driving home in his green Saab 9-3. As the early evening dusk was taking over, he switched on his headlights, illuminating the road ahead. Suddenly, a 4x4 Toyota behind him flashed their bright headlights, dazzling him through the rear-view mirror.

'Bloody morons.' He adjusted the mirror as the 4x4 continued to keep their headlights on full. He slowed down and pulled over in the gateway of a field so the morons could overtake. As they moved up alongside, he flipped the V's to the male passenger in the front seat. The passenger just laughed back at him as he pulled down a balaclava over his face.

The Toyota swerved and came to a stop, blocking his Saab. Three masked figures in dark clothing jumped out and approached at full pelt. One smashed the driver's window with a hammer. Frightened, he tried to shield his head from the flying shattered glass. It covered the interior of the car; fragments were nicking his skin on his face and hands. Blood started to trickle.

Another seized the door and nearly wrenched it off its hinges. A knife threatening in hand, they cut the seat belt and dragged him out of the car. Forced him to the ground. He screamed as he felt the vicious attack of kicks on every part of his body. A foot hovered over his ankle before it came down forcefully. Crying out in pain, he felt his ankle crack. More kicks followed, to his ribs, to his abdomen. Agony speared through him.

After what seemed like forever, the beating stopped. Instead, he felt their hands on his legs and arms as they bound it with tape and dragged him to the rear of his car. He saw through swollen eyes and the haze of blood coating his face the boot being opened. Hands on his arms and legs again and he was lifted, then dumped into the boot. From his dark, cramped cell, he heard someone get into the car and start the engine. The car drove off.

Desperate, he tried to undo the ties. To no avail. His fingers were numbed and his body ached all over, every movement agony.

The car stopped. He heard movement outside, gravel being crunched. Muffled talking. Through the bulkhead of the rear seats, he heard the rear door open. A pungent smell hit his nostrils, Petrol.

'HELP. GET ME OUT', he shouted. Pain racked his ribs and lungs.

Smelling burning fabric, he started coughing as smoke infiltrated the boot. Choking, he kicked out at the boot's lock.

Soon, the smoke and heat became too much.

His last breath burned his throat.

Acknowledgements

I would like to thank Caroline and Jon at City Stone Publishing for their hard work in publishing this book. They have made me feel very welcome, and I am happy to work with them.

I would also like to thank Ross Greenwood for the invitation to Dark Side Of Fiction, and for bouncing off ideas regarding the prison parts of this book. To Maureen Davis and Beryl Fielder for their help as BETA readers.

To Kerrie Watson and Kerry Monteith. The original Watson & Monteith. It was a pleasure working with you.

Finally, I would like to thank you, my readers. Thank you for purchasing this book. I hope you enjoyed it. Please, leave a review on Amazon, Goodreads or any of the other review sites.

Regards,

Tony

About the Author

Tony Millington is the author of the *Ravenswood Crime Series*, currently comprising five books. Set in the fictional city of Ravenswood, DCI Watson and his sidekick, DS Monteith, are the lead detectives of the city's police force.

Prior to writing, Tony spent many years as a civil servant in the MOD, working on local RAF bases. Also, he worked for the local council in Adult and Children's Social Care. He originates from Cheshire, and moved down to Rutland when he was thirteen. He now lives in Cambridgeshire and has been happily married for over twenty-six years; the couple has a son.

Tony volunteers as a facilitator in Peterborough for AMC (Andy's Man Club) charity, a men's suicide prevention charity.

When not writing and walking his Romanian rescue dog, Mira, or catering to the demands of his cat Lucky, you can find Tony rocking out to heavy metal.

Tony Millington on social media:
Facebook: TonyMillingtonAuthor
Twitter: @TonyMillington9

About City Stone Publishing

Indie publisher with a passion for the written word
and a heart that beats for authors everywhere

We are an imaginative and enthusiastic indie publisher.

Our ambition is twofold:

To develop outstanding books and work alongside our authors.

To be a beacon of advice and a provider of services for indie authors.

We are not just about the books; we build relationships with our authors. Because we both write, we know what (indie) authors want. That is how we work: in cooperation and partnership with our authors.

From dark and gritty crime thrillers, adventurous fantasy, entertaining women's fiction, and intriguing contemporary novels to interesting and insightful non-fiction and visionary poetry, we publish it all.

Visit our website: citystonepublishing.com

About AMC

ANDYSMANCLUB are a men's suicide prevention charity, offering free-to-attend peer-to-peer support groups across the United Kingdom and online.

Their goal is to end the stigma surrounding men's mental health and help men through the power of conversation.

ANDYSMANCLUB want to eliminate the stigma surrounding mental health and create a judgment-free, confidential space where men can be open about the storms in their lives.

They aim to achieve this through weekly, free-to-attend peer-to-peer support groups for men aged over 18.

#ITSOKAYTOTALK
www.andysmanclub.co.uk

Milton Keynes UK
Ingram Content Group UK Ltd.
UKHW012014290224
438689UK00001B/35